my imperfect Love Story

my imperfect Love Story

Shubhashish Kerketta

Srishti
Publishers & Distributors

Srishti Publishers & Distributors
A unit of AJR Publishing LLP
212A, Peacock Lane
Shahpur Jat, New Delhi – 110 049
editorial@srishtipublishers.com

First published by
Srishti Publishers & Distributors in 2021

10 9 8 7 6 5 4 3 2 1

Printed and bound in India

Dedicated to

all those who love and never give up.

Acknowledgement

Before everyone else, I would like to thank the almighty god for giving me the strength to complete this novel.

The journey of more than eighteen months has been absolutely enthralling. It pushed me off the cliff to take a deep dive into introspection and self-discovery. The task at hand seemed to be daunting initially and the finish line was miles away.

However, once I began this enriching journey, there was no stopping and looking back. I cannot take all the credit alone as it has been a collective endeavour. There are a number of loving souls who helped me get through the days of frustration and creative blocks while penning down the story.

I would like to extend my heartfelt gratitude to my family – my mother Argen Kerketta, my better half Priya and my sister Yognisha for being a solid support throughout the process. R (you know it) for reading my raw drafts and giving me invaluable inputs to make it better. My friends who helped me unconditionally through this journey.

Arup, Stuti and the entire team of Srishti for showing faith in my work and being wonderful, right from the beginning till the end. You all have painstakingly honed my work and shared the best version of *My Imperfect Love Story* with the world.

And finally, I would like to thank all the readers who are holding this book in their hands. I am sure you all are geared up to rediscover the power of your love. I hope to surpass your expectations!

1

Happy New Year?

1 January 2019

Midnight

A new year is always an exciting experience. It feels like an exquisite bouquet of vibrant flowers fragrant with joy, hope, love, success and better health. It's yet another chance for us to take a step towards becoming a better version of ourselves.

As the day approached again this year, millions of heads were abuzz with a list of New Year resolutions or brand new to-do lists. It was that three hundred and sixty fifth night and yet, I sat on my bed and stared out of the window.

The ambience was brimming with energy, thanks to the various stage performances, bright and colourful lights and hullabaloos from the televisions of folks who preferred to celebrate within the four walls of their sweet homes. The sky was lit up jubilantly; gangs of people of all ages were moving around like excited, buzzing bees.

There was a sudden rise in the uproar and the sky turned multihued, making a major announcement, "Happy New Year 2019!"

My eyes were roaming through the benign sky when the most peaceful of the voices lured them back. "Happy new year, Amy!"

It was my mom – the woman who had brought me up single-handedly after my dad passed away in an accident at his workplace while I was still in school. The ex-gratia compensation made by the company was wisely invested by her to build this small house that we live in today. She worked as a teacher in a convent school, which was also my alma mater, and took tuitions in the evening. The amount of sacrifice that she might have made in her life was beyond my comprehension.

"Happy new year, mama!" I got up and hugged her tight. "I thought you would have slept by now."

"I wanted to be the first one to wish you," she said while kissing my forehead and combing my hair with her fingers.

A ripple of serenity traversed through me as I was engulfed by her love. "I love you, mom," I whispered.

"I love you too," she replied most affectionately.

It is an eternal truth that a mother's love is pure and endowed with magical powers that can mend even the most brutally broken hearts. She wishes to be our best friend, but we choose to lie, cheat and undermine her continually, until we come face to face with chaos.

Bzzt… bzzt… My phone started vibrating, flashing the name "Oli".

I took the call and shouted, "Happy new year, Oli!"

"Happy new year," she squealed in delight.

"What's up?" I asked.

"Just watching some live shows on my phone. What about you?" she asked in her naturally soft dulcet tone.

"I was sitting with mom."

"Is aunty still awake?"

"Yes!"

"Put the phone on speaker."

I did and said, "She can hear you."

"Happy new year, aunty!" she wished her respectfully.

"Happy new year, child. God bless you!"

"Thank you, aunty."

"Is Tara awake?" Mom asked.

"No, mom is probably in the ninth or tenth dimension at this hour." She chuckled.

"No problem! I will talk to her in the morning."

"Sure aunty," she replied.

"Okay children, I will leave the two of you. This old body is in desperate need of some tenth dimension stuff," Mom said jokingly.

She kissed me goodnight and left the room.

"I think we should get some sleep now. Our talks shall never get over," Oli said lazily and yawned twice before reaching the end of her sentence after two hours of long gossip.

"Okay sleepy head—"

I was speaking when she interrupted me, "By the way, I needed to show you something!"

"What?" I asked curiously.

"Come over to my place tomorrow morning."

"Okay! What is it about?"

"Just come and see it for yourself, Amy," she said.

"Uff!" I answered in an irritated tone.

The world had grown dark and quiet by then. I, Amyra – better known as Amy by my loved ones – looked outside the window; this time to see myself in the panes. There is absolutely nothing special about me. I have always been an average student (scoring in the line of fifties and sixties) with an extreme phobia of mathematics, carrying an average look, devoid of any talent that would set me apart. However, I have always been proud of two things; one is my height and the other, my deep brown eyes.

At present, I am in the first year of my post-graduation from St. Agnes College, Bangalore. Ranchi is my home. I had stepped into my sweet home just a few hours ago, to be with my mom for New Year's Eve.

The long conversation with my *chuddy-buddy* suddenly stirred up a myriad of memories that lay hidden in the trenches of my mind. My mind took me to my twenty-first birthday; the day Shashank spoke to me for the first time.

2

Twenty-Onederful

30 September 2016

Midnight

Bzzt… Bzzt… Bzzt… My phone was vibrating continually, flashing the name "Piu".

I received and got connected to the conference call with my two besties, Piu and Oli.

"Hello!" I said.

"Happy birthday to you, happy birthday to you, may god bless you… Many boyfriends to you, happy birthday to you, Amy!" They sang the most cacophonic birthday song ever in the history of singing, but I enjoyed every bit of it with a big smile.

"Thank you!" I said gleefully and blew kisses over the phone.

The first step to my twenty-first birthday had been with two of my favourite people and I did not wish it to be any better.

Priyanka Singh and Olive Ekka, better known by their nicknames Piu and Oli, had been by my side since the days I used to shit in my pants (so did they!).

Our houses were within five minutes' walk from each other's. We went to the same school, same class and even the same section throughout. Many around us had seen us growing up together in school and then college.

We shared approximately the same height and complexion. Oli was the quietest, while Piu's lips were completely ignorant of full stops or commas.

Oli was a gifted artist who made stunning pencil sketches, apart from amazing hair styles and makeup. She had been the knight in shining armour since our school days for our project works that required a hell lot of drawings. Her mom worked as a sales woman in a garment shop while her father was an office assistant in a local construction company.

Piu was the prettiest and also the smartest in our group, who had a clear solution to every problem on her fingertips. Her mother was a teacher in a play school and also an insurance agent. She was just four years old when her father succumbed to meningitis.

The three of us had taken admission in the English department of St. Louis College, Ranchi (popularly known as SLCR).

Now, SLCR was a top-ranked co-ed college, but not a single boy had taken admission in our department in the last two years. It was, and still is, a mystery if there weren't any male applicants at all or we were just the victims of some eerie plot that prohibited them from applying to our faculty.

Whatever the case might have been, the vacuum which was created attracted many boys from other departments, flouting the rules sometimes, leading to frequent interventions by our professors.

The faculty of English was rechristened "World of Angels" (abbreviated as WOA) by the students of other departments, who strolled around our corridor uselessly, trying to stalk some or the other girl. Some of the girls of our class led them on, resulting in even more chaos.

As per my observation and calculation (which can be trusted, considering it had both Piu and Oli's backing), it was just the three of us who formed an unmitigated girl gang both inside and outside the class.

Our gossip of over ninety minutes revolved around our college and my birthday plans. I was super excited for my birthday, as always, even though there had never been anything like a big celebration until then.

9:05 a.m.

My first class for the day was due in forty minutes and I was still struggling to get into my clothes. Piu and Oli were already home. They were busy nibbling the *kachoris* served by mom, least concerned about getting late for the class.

I joined them and mom's phone rang.

"Hello," she said and handed the phone to me saying, "It's Shaila aunty!"

I rolled my eyes and said while munching, "Hello aunty!"

"Hello Amy, wish you a very happy birthday, kid!" she said in the most fabricated voice.

"Thank you aunty," I replied in the same way, making faces.

"Talk to your uncle!" she said.

'I don't wanna talk to any of you guys!' I thought, but by that time, his monotonous voice took a speck of life out of my vibrant day, "Hello Amy! Happy birthday. God bless you."

"Thanks!" I said, trying to conceal my irritation.

"Hello Amy! What's the plan for the day?" It was her again. He had either given the phone back to aunty without saying so or she took it by force. *Weirdos*!

"Nothing, I am getting late for the college aunty. Will catch up with you later. Bye!" I said and disconnected the call without waiting for her reply.

That felt damn good; just like slamming the door on her face and even breaking her nose. An evil smile spread across my face.

Newton's third law of motion states, "Every action has an equal and opposite reaction." Just like that, mom had comprehended my action and it was time for her reaction.

"Is this the way you talk to your aunt?" she asked angrily.

"Maa, please don't do this on my birthday!" I said, trying to put on my best puppy-eyes face.

"That's not gonna work. I haven't taught you to disrespect elders," she said in an upset tone.

"Okay! I am sorry, mom. I will talk to her in the evening. But you know that I hate her," I was irritated and continued. "Bye mom!"

I took my stuff and darted out of the house, while my friends showed up outside only after a minute. They must have got some instructions from my mom to make me understand the importance of moral values.

I never understood why mom needed to cajole them. She was the very same Shaila aunty who, along with her husband, tried to get her hands on all the money that we received from the company after dad's death. In fact, the only reason that she came for the funeral and stayed back at our home (unlike all other relatives who showed up for formality sake and left the two bereaved ladies alone) was to manipulate my emotionally disturbed mom into giving away the gratuity and insurance amounts for the fulfilment of their loan and other liabilities. Coincidentally, I overheard them at night and informed mom, which ruined their well-laid plan to rob us.

9:45 a.m.

We reached the class on the dot. The girls looked at us expectantly, thinking it was the show stopper, Prof Shashank Raj. They dropped their heads in disappointment the very next moment.

Loaded with the burden of their disappointments, we yanked our sorry selves to the usual bench in the second last row.

The girls stood up the moment we sat down and chirped, "Good morning, sir!"

The three of us got up clumsily.

"Good morning, girls," he replied in his usual buoyant style.

Prof Shashank Raj, the youngest faculty member in college was in his mid-twenties, reaching over six-feet tall and sporting a sturdy physique that revealed his six-pack abs from over his shirt. He had dark brown eyes, wheatish complexion and a soft yet sturdy voice. His gentle, helpful nature and heart-throbbing personality made him an excellent teacher.

Every girl in our faculty, whether committed or single, had a huge crush on him. He had always been a hot topic of discussion among girls.

As for me, I missed a heartbeat every time my eyes caught a glimpse of him. I was smitten with every little detail – the way he walked, the way he talked, the way he taught, the way he dressed, the way he sang, the way he played guitar, and so on… I can go on and on.

He was Shashank sir for the rest of the class, but for me, he was only 'Shashank'.

My eyes were fixed on him as he stood right at the centre, dressed in a navy blue shirt and black trousers. His sleeves were rolled up, revealing his stylish light tanned leather strap watch. The brown leather belt and a matching pair of formal shoes just added to my drooling over him.

I knew he was completely out of my league, yet I did not want to quit without a fight. Silly me!

The girls sighed as he walked elegantly towards the podium and took our attendance. I was busy enjoying a hot date with him in my trance that was rudely interrupted by Oli, who pinched my arm.

I looked at her and asked, "What?"

"You missed your attendance," she replied.

"Oh!" I said and waited for him to reach the end.

Then, I raised my hand and said, "Roll number thirty-one, sir."

He looked at me and asked smilingly, "What were you dreaming about, Amyra? Would you like to share with us?"

I blushed in the middle of the class and dropped my gaze to my feet. "Nothing sir. I was just flipping through the pages of my book," I murmured softly.

He smiled, marked my attendance and started his lecture. My eyes followed him, whereas my mind helplessly fluttered along untravelled roads with fancy dreams of him. The class of forty-five minutes was over in a jiffy.

"Amyra, come and meet me in the staffroom," he said before leaving.

"Okay, sir!" I responded reflexively as numerous jealous eyes turned towards me.

"What the hell?" I thought to myself, "Shit! Did he catch me checking him out?"

"Come with me!" I said, looking at my two personal bodyguards.

"Go Amy, go! We don't wanna be playing gooseberry!" They winked.

I pulled them up and they finally joined me for the critical mission 'Meet Shashank'.

By the time we reached the staff room, my mind had expeditiously created a new feeling by blending excitement, doubt, embarrassment, reluctance, fear and joy.

Shashank was checking his phone when I asked, "May I come in, sir?"

"Oh yes, please come in!" he said.

Everything about this man seemed so sophisticated, including his cubicle. A miniature paddle rickshaw woven out of copper wires made up his pen stand alongside a set of wooden tea coasters with some quotes written on them. The books and papers were neatly arranged on the side too.

"Happy birthday, Amyra!" He wished me and extended his hand for a shake.

I stretched out my hand clumsily. Goosebumps emerged all over my body as I shook his warm, strong and mildly rough hand for a few moments until he withdrew. I stood there, grinning like an idiot as he took out a chocolate.

"This is for you," he said with a smile.

"But sir—"

I was interrupted by him, "C'mon, take it!"

I struggled hard to keep my feet on the ground in elation. "Okay! Thank you so much, sir. How did you know about my birthday?"

"The top right corner on Facebook revealed your birthday this morning," he replied with a soft chuckle.

I had nervously sent him a friend request the day before with zero expectations.

"Thank you for accepting it, sir." I smiled.

"You're welcome! C'mon now, your next class is due in three minutes. I think you should rush," he said.

"Yes sir," I said and left the staffroom in haste.

I could not wait to share this exciting info with my two besties.

"Oh my god!" The girls screamed in excitement as I flaunted the Dairy Milk Silk chocolate that was concealed in my dupatta.

"Shhhh…" I hushed them and they covered their mouths.

We hurried towards our classroom. However, this episode had triggered strange thoughts in me. 'Has he been noticing me? Why would he, there's nothing special about me! Numerous pretty, hot, sexy, brilliant and talented girls would line up for him. But then, why did he give me a chocolate? I don't think he gives such a delectable present to all the girls in his Facebook friend list on their birthdays. Does he like me?' The mere idea kicked butterflies in my stomach.

We reached the classroom and I placed myself on the bench mechanically, engrossed in the garden of my contemplation.

10:30 p.m.

I was enjoying my solitude in bed in the last few hours of my twenty-first birthday. A big smile rested on my face as I played the exciting events of the day in my mind.

The three of us had stepped into my house, completely exhausted after battling through several lectures in the college at around five in the evening.

I did not get any more wishes from anyone (and there wasn't any need whatsoever). Perhaps my small world was confined to my mother, two of my friends and the latest entrant, Shashank. My faithful friends had been by my side throughout the day. Mom had invited Kunal uncle, who was accompanied by his wife Megha aunty and two of her colleagues with their families for dinner apart from my friends' mothers.

The cake-cutting ceremony began at around eight as I enacted the ritual of making a wish before blowing the candles, brimming with excitement like a small kid.

"I want to be with Shashank!" I shut my eyes firmly and prayed zealously.

"Happy birthday to you... Happy birthday to you..." A group of people closest to my heart started singing and clapping, the moment I opened my eyes and blew out the candles.

I cut the cake and put a piece in everyone's mouth one by one. The three of us utilised the icing on the cake carefully to smear a small part of our cheeks as a formality. However, it transformed into a lavish creamy Holi party soon. No one was spared that evening. It was the first birthday bash of my life and I was on top of the world.

It was followed by a sumptuous dinner with peas *pulao*, chicken curry, *papad* and *raita*. All of us relished our food, until our tummies were about to burst while chit-chatting about different topics.

The best part was the dumb charade game. The frenzied imagination of aunties and the amusing gestures used by uncles were unparalleled. Our faces beamed with joy as we rolled with laughter.

I was thoroughly enjoying my voyage down the memory lane, when my phone beeped.

'Who could it be?' I thought while searching for it lazily all over my bed with my hand. Finally, I found it hidden deep within my bed sheet. My eyes that were turning heavy with exhaustion, suddenly became lighter than a feather as soon as I checked the text.

It was from Shashank. *What's up, birthday girl?*

I could not believe my eyes. I checked the sender's name multiple times to believe it. My heart started pumping blood heavily all over my body to activate every organ, especially my eyes and brain. I typed and retyped about ten times before finalising my response. After taking some deep breaths, I pinged, *Nothing sir, just came to bed. What about you?*

Beep.

Me too. His response came almost immediately.

Beep.

How did you celebrate your special day?

I replied, *It was good sir. We had a small family get together at home.*

Wow! That's great.

Yes sir… I typed, not knowing what more to say.

So, am I qualified enough to get a treat from u? He wrote with a wink.

His words were magical; violins played in my ears as I read that line. I whispered, "You are qualified for many more things Shashank!" and quickly typed, *Sure sir.*

I was just kidding, Amyra.

"No, you weren't," I said to myself and dropped him some emojis, showing that I was upset at his reply.

What happened?

Nothing, I replied, praying that he did not think me to be a despo!

Okay! Sorry… so when are you treating me? He pinged with a smiley.

The reply brought a smile back to my lips. *Whenever you say, sir*!

How about tomorrow? It's a Saturday and a holiday for both of us.

That's if you don't have any other plans.

Two continuous messages made me nervous. I really wanted to go out with him, but the very next day was too early. I could not have gone out with him, looking like his pet chimpanzee. Reluctantly, I lied, *Sir, I have to go to the hospital with my mother tomorrow. Can we meet on Sunday?*

A heavy stone of regret rolled over my heart as numerous apprehensions rushed in. I started praying hastily, "Please god, don't let him drop the plan. Let him be free on Sunday. Please, please, please."

I got my answer pretty soon.

Okay cool, we will meet on Sunday.

I sighed with relief and thanked the almighty for answering my prayer while typing, *Sure sir!*

We will decide the time and venue later.

Okay sir, I typed.

My eyes are very heavy, Amyra.

Good night

"Please no! I am not done yet. I want to talk more. Please don't go Shashank," I said and typed, *Good night sir*.

He read my text and went offline. Sleep evaded me after that. I was thrilled and wanted to share this happiness with my friends. I called Piu and she answered drowsily, "Hello!"

I said, "Hold on, I will take Oli in conference."

"Let us hope it is something important," she said while yawning.

"It is!" I said and put her on hold to call Oli.

"Hello girls, I have to tell you something really exciting," I said.

"Make it quick! I am in full sleep mode," Piu said droopily.

"Shashank wants to go out with me!" I shouted frantically.

There was a quick shift in their voices from sleepy to thrill as they exclaimed, "What! Really?"

I could not help but imagine them spring up in their beds with their eyes wide open. Within a second, they started bombarding me with numerous questions all at once which got so chaotic that I heard none.

I said, "Guys, just listen!"

After a few seconds of anxious hearsay, they finally stopped.

There was a moment of absolute silence which was broken by Oli, "Tell us the details!"

3

My First (Unofficial) Date!

2 October 2016

9:00 a.m.

The day before had been one of the longest Saturdays of my life. My friends stayed with me after lunch as we prepared a master plan to hide my outing with him for the next day. There was not a slightest chance that mom would have allowed me to go out with Shashank (or as a matter of fact, any guy). They also pampered me like a bride-to-be for the next day. They gave me a pearl facial, waxed my hands and legs, and gave me a relaxing manicure and pedicure. Shashank confirmed our meeting in the City Centre mall at eleven by evening.

Piu, the smartest one, came up with the superb idea of us stepping out of our houses together like we were going for a movie at the same mall. Then, I would meet Shashank, whereas they would go for a movie or window shopping. We just needed to ensure that we reached back to our houses together to avoid any suspicion.

And there it was – the day of my first unofficial date! Mom was surprised to see my liveliness that morning. That definitely was a positive side effect of love. A *sloth* had turned to a *beaver*.

I put on my new white and pink printed top with black denims and was all geared up by 8.30 a.m., waiting impatiently for Piu. She reached my house after a gruelling wait of thirty minutes. I had already called her five times by then.

We reached Oli's home in the next five minutes. She was busy ironing her light blue shirt that she was going to put on with black denims. She was in no hurry as we had plans of getting ready there. Thankfully, her mom wasn't home, giving us an ample opportunity to wear all the makeup we wanted.

Oli styled my hair in soft waves using her curler and announced proudly, "He won't be able to look anywhere else."

"I don't think that's the only place she wants him to see," Piu said naughtily.

I blushed and they laughed.

Then, they painted my face with BB cream, mascara, eyeliner, lipstick, lip liner and other such stuff. Oli gave me a set of matching earrings, ring and a bracelet.

I fell in love with myself as I looked in the mirror. They had done a great job and I thanked them with kisses.

We left the house and took an auto-rickshaw. An inexplicable nervousness dominated me as the brightly-coloured mall painted its picture in my eyes.

I was lost in my own world as we stepped inside. Piu and Oli were busy planning their day. They had a lot of time to spare as they had already booked their tickets online for the noon show.

My phone rang; it was him. "Hey Amy! Where are you?"

"City Centre, sir," I replied.

"I am just near the gate," he said.

"Okay sir. I will be… there… in a minute." I was already out of breath.

"Relax Amyra, and walk easily. I am not going anywhere without you," he said.

A pinch of mischief was sprinkled in his calm voice which made me feel better. I reached the gate soon and saw him standing beside his black sedan car. Nobody could have missed him. He was wearing a mauve shirt and grey trousers with a black leather belt, brown shoes and aviator sunglasses.

Damn! He looked so hot.

A lot of girls were checking him out, whereas he waited for *me*. The thought made me swell. I took a moment to check myself in one of the car's window before dropping on him.

"Good morning sir!" I said, from behind.

"Good morning, pretty lady," he replied with a big heart-warming smile as he turned towards me.

"Wow! How many guys did you see falling around you today?" he asked naughtily.

"Not even one!" I said, trying hard to conceal my happiness.

"You look gorgeous," he said.

"Thank you sir." I blushed and the worse happened, he noticed it.

"Please get into my humble wagon," the gentleman said and opened the door for me.

A special feeling plugged into my heart as I entered the car and sat down clumsily. He closed the door and went to the other side to take the driver's seat. His 'humble wagon' exhibited an intense lush feel inside.

I looked at the road straight out of the windshield as he drove us out of the busy main road area. It was hard for me to believe that I was actually going out with Shashank. From the corner of my eyes, I could see the black steering with numerous buttons, and his hands. They looked sturdy and strong. His Xylys watch added to the glory.

"So, where do you want to go, one-day-old baby?" He stressed on the last few words.

He used the 'baby' word pretty smartly. However, I did not mind it. Rather, I loved it. I was tempted to use the same word.

"I don't know sir, wherever you want," I said trying to choose the right words.

"It's your treat, so you have the option," he said.

"I don't go out to the restaurants sir, so…" I said.

"Okay chill, I'll take you to the place of my choice," he said before I could complete my sentence.

"Okay sir," I said while a plethora of thoughts ran through my mind. 'Where is he planning to take me? I hope I could afford treating him there.'

The thoughts of all possible embarrassing scenarios made me nervous.

My thoughts were interrupted by his voice, "Where are you lost? Is everything okay?"

"Yes. It's just that I have never been out with anyone alone." I uttered those words and thought, 'Shit! What did I just say?'

"Don't worry, you are not alone in it. Even I haven't been out with anyone for years," he said laughingly.

4

The Oracle

Whoa! My jaw dropped as I looked at the structure in front of me. It was a beautiful restaurant named The Oracle.

The two-storey building that stood amidst a beautiful garden was painted aesthetically in a combination of white, light green, maroon and gold. The garden was teeming with beautiful flowers and ornamental plants. There was a lawn and an open-air restaurant with multihued garden umbrellas.

'Fuck! I can't treat him here.' I thought anxiously.

He sensed my anxiety immediately and said, "Don't you worry girl, the treat is on me. But, an ice-cream treat from you would be due."

I said, "But we had planned for my birthday tr—"

"Sshh!" he stopped me and asked for my hand, just like in movies.

I was embarrassed, excited, confused, enlivened and a bit angry; all emotions were overwhelming me one after the other. It was natural for any girl to experience a surge of emotions at such an instance.

Almost immediately, I put my palm on his. A wave of exhilaration passed through my entire body as he held my hand and we walked towards the restaurant like a couple.

A well-dressed person in white and red greeted and opened the door for us.

Shashank smiled at him while I didn't know what to do then. It was my first experience of going inside a posh restaurant and I felt like a monkey that had accidentally entered a sophisticated place.

The entire hall was divided into two parts by way of painted designer translucent glasses, lit with pastel lights. The front segment had neatly arranged tables and chairs while the posterior segment had cubicles for people who preferred privacy.

The inside was brushed superbly in dark brown and golden and was dimly lit. The ambience kicked in some notorious ideas in my mind. While I was busy appreciating the beauty of the place, Shashank had drawn me to one of the cubicles. I realized what he was up to when I heard his voice, "After you."

I came out of the trance awkwardly and stepped in mechanically. He followed me inside and took a seat right in front of me after offering the chair to me.

The interiors of the cubicle was especially luxurious. A medium-sized wooden table was positioned in the centre with four chairs (two on either side).

The sudden awkward silence was broken by Shashank, "Where are you lost?"

"Nowhere sir, just admiring the place." I continued, "I have never been to a place like this before. Everything looks so neat and perfect. I am in love with this place."

'And much more with you,' I thought in continuance.

He looked straight into my eyes.

'Shit! Did he read my mind?'

That assumption made me conscious, and I started flipping the pages of the menu book.

"Someone is very hungry," he said with a grin on his face.

Now, that was embarrassing. I closed it and said, "No sir. I was just checking out the exotic names in the menu."

"Is it?" he said innocently.

"Please don't act ignorant, sir. You must have come here like a hundred times?" I replied.

"That's way too high a number." He grinned.

He then, picked up the menu on his side and we started exploring the complicated and jazzy names mentioned in it.

One of the items said, "Crispy fried cover with savoury fillings served with organic tamarind."

"Does this even mean anything?" I asked laughingly.

"It is nothing but two *samosas* served with *imli chutney*," he replied with a big smile.

"Whoa... Really..." My eyes widened, ready to pop out of my sockets.

"A few days back, my cousins brought me samosas from here, and the bill said the exact same thing that's written here."

"Okay," I said, thinking about the crispy fried which we call *singhara* and get at ten rupees near our homes.

"And what's this?" I asked pointing at something that said, "Pan roasted pastry rolls, layered with tomato puree and herbs, blend with cheese and soft aged salami."

He looked at it inquisitively and after a minute of serious investigation he said, "It's the last line of Shakespeare's last drama that nobody ever got a chance to see!" We immediately burst into uncontrollable laughter at his words.

We continued our game of making fun of flowery names as our laughter filled the cubicle. I was enjoying every moment with the man whom I loved, from the first day that I saw him – the man of my dreams. He had a beautiful smile, just like that of an innocent kid.

Our conversation was paused by a call from his mother. He started talking to her, while I excused myself to visit the restroom. I reached after a few minutes to find him using his phone.

"Hey, let's order something or else these people may kick us out!" He giggled as I settled.

Our survey to find the best food from a complex web of jargons began soon.

We collectively zeroed down to the starters, the main course and the desserts with the help of a man who was wearing a white shirt and black suit with a bow in his collar. (I saw one after years) He readily came when Shashank signalled him for help.

He took out a notepad with golden cover from his coat's pocket and a black pen to jot down our order after saving us from drowning into the ocean of incomprehensible food jargon. His rich vocabulary and grammatically impeccable sentences had already put me to shame. I chose to be quiet to avoid making a fool of myself.

Shashank placed the order, while asking for my preferences, as I stared at the two English gurus.

The man left soon and Shashank turned his attention to me for the first time in the last three minutes. He asked, "Do you have a boyfriend?"

The question came unexpectedly, from out of nowhere.

"No sir!" The reply came out in a matter-of-fact way as I looked down and blushed. I tried to hide my bashful smile from him, but was that even possible!

"Okay," he said

I could sense respite in his voice, or maybe I was reading into it too much.

"Do you, sir?" Now, these words again came out abruptly without my intention. My heart had taken control over my thoughts, words and actions.

I could see a sudden change in his facial expressions. His eyebrows suddenly rose.

"Sorry sir! I did not mean to intrude into your personal space," I said apologetically.

"No, no! Don't be! It's perfectly fine." He said, "I had a girlfriend long back when I was pursuing my graduation."

"Why did you guys break up, sir?" It seemed rather strange that any girl would ever break up with a guy like him.

He looked away from me momentarily and replied, "We didn't. She ditched me."

That came as a shocker.

'How can a girl ditch someone like him for anyone else in the world?' I thought to myself, 'She must have been insane.'

But it's good that she left him. Otherwise I wouldn't be sitting here with him. The thought kicked off a bitchy smile on my lips that I concealed cautiously.

I brought a fake expression on my face and said, "I am sorry to hear that, sir. Maybe you deserved better than her."

Only, I knew that the better I just mentioned here was *me*.

"I am over it, dear," he said and looked straight into my eyes.

I turned red again and looked down.

He continued, "There has been nobody in my life since then, just my best friend Anurag. He has been with me in all ups and downs in my life. He was actually the one who helped me get over Ritu."

'Thanks a lot, Ritu,' I shouted in my mind.

"May I come in, sir?" A waiter knocked.

"Yes!" Shashank replied.

The next ninety minutes of our lives were spent in consuming thousands of calories that were served to us through a series of starters, main course and desserts.

Furthermore, I got a better glimpse into his life; both past and present. He was pursuing his Ph.D from Ranchi University, just to be with his mother, when he could have easily got an admission anywhere in India, owing to his excellent performance in the NET examination.

He also shared a few details of his incomplete love story. They had been together for approximately two-and-a-half years when he was pursuing his graduation from St. Stephen's College, Delhi – one of the best colleges in India.

She had proposed after the first semester results when he had been the topper and stopped talking to him abruptly for no reason soon after the completion of their final semester examination. He tried to get in touch with her in his bewilderment, but she did not let that happen. He met her in college only during the convocation, where she blatantly informed him that she was already seeing someone else.

Later, he also came to know from their common friends that she had been with him just for popularity and academic gains. He was a vocalist and guitarist who had represented his college and won many accolades in a number of competitions. Apart from that, he had a very good rapport with both the seniors and the professors. Ritu took advantage of all his connections in the most effective way.

He did not tell me about the depth of their relationship and I was afraid to know more. A wave of sympathy engulfed my heart as he narrated his story.

'All he needs is pure selfless love and I am going to pour all my affection on him if he accepts me!' I made a promise to myself that day.

As far as I was concerned, I told him a lot of things about my little world comprising my mother, my best friends and no boyfriend ever. I did tell him in detail about my dad and my family.

Time had flown by in a jiffy as I looked at my phone that said, 'You need to get going, Amyra!'

It was close to 4:30 p.m. when he stopped the car at one of the parking spaces a few meters away from the mall.

"Please stretch out your hand, Amyra!"

"Sir?" I looked at him blankly.

"I said, please stretch out your hand," he repeated.

I did that reluctantly as I did not want to accept a gift from him. He had already spent a lot by giving me a treat on my birthday.

He took something out from the glove compartment and placed it in my palms, "Happy birthday, Amyra!"

I was speechless as my eyes sparkled at the sight of a magnificent peach-coloured bracelet.

"Sir... but—"

"I know it's not that good, but I tried my best..."

"It's not that, sir. It's gorgeous," I said, succumbing to his emotional blackmail.

"Then keep it! It's for you," he said.

I had no option left. "Thank you very much, sir!"

"I think it would match well with your dress," he said looking at me intently.

"Would you..." I put the bracelet in his palm and stretched my hand towards him after removing the one that I was wearing.

He hooked it around my wrist perfectly as my cheeks turned crimson.

"You should call your friends," he said while pointing at his watch.

"Yes," I said and dialled Piu.

5

He Loves Me

It had been three months since I had my first informal conversation with Shashank and things changed drastically from then. He changed from an unattainable dream to an indispensible part of my life in the days and nights that followed. A few minutes without his text or call made me restless and I started to believe he also felt the same. We were already in a relationship even though we didn't acknowledge it. I wanted to open my heart to him on numerous occasions, but backed out each time. I really wanted him to take the first step.

I could not spend time with Oli and Piu like before (due to obvious reasons), but they seemed to be okay with the change. The best part was that the freshness of our friendship was completely unaffected by his entry.

31 December 2016

10:00 a.m.

It was the last day of the leap year 2016 and all our classmates were enjoying the winter vacations thoroughly, except me!

I craved for a single glimpse of Shashank. Thanks to technology for handing us the video call facility. It came as a life saver every day after mom left and at nights after she dozed off.

It was around ten in the morning when I got the routine video call from Shashank.

"Hi!" I waved in excitement the moment he appeared after a few seconds of buffering.

"Hey!" He waved back. "What's up?"

"Nothing, just completed some household chores."

"Hmm! Turning into a homemaker!" He winked.

I blushed and said, "No!"

"Okay, so what plans for the evening?"

"Nothing yet," I replied.

"In that case, don't plan anything else. I got passes for us to celebrate New Year's Eve at The Meltdown," he said.

The Meltdown was yet another top-notch hotel in the city that I had never dared to enter.

The sound of this name in itself got me on the edge and I shouted, "Wow!"

The very next moment, a blunt reality dawned on me and made me recoil back to the centre. "What would I say to mom?" I said drearily.

"Don't worry Amy! I took passes for Piu and Oli also. I hope they are free," he said.

His thoughtful action brought a bright smile back to my face and I said, "Okay, I'll ask them and get back to you."

Once we had spoken and disconnected, I took Piu and Oli in a conference call. "Hey guys, Shashank got passes for new year celebration in The Meltdown. Are you free?" I said in a single breath.

"Yes!" Piu was thrilled and replied without wasting a split second.

"I am free, but what would we say at home?" Oli asked, worried.

"We will plan something. Can't afford to miss it!" Piu said excitedly.

"Yes," I added.

"Okay, if you guys say so... I am in," Oli said in a confused voice. She was hesitant, but we knew she won't back out; she never did.

"Okay guys, I'll talk to you later. Get ready for some late night action," I said.

I called Shashank right away. He responded at the first ring, as if waiting for me with the phone in his hand.

"Hello sir. They are free," I said.

"That's good! I will pick you girls at around nine in the evening?" he said.

"Okay, we will be ready by then," I said eagerly.

"Chalo, I have to go now. Will see you later," he said.

"Are you busy, sir?" I asked sadly.

"Yeah, I have some guests over. Will catch up with you later."

"Okay sir. Bye," I said reluctantly.

We didn't talk much that day, but he had given me a solid reason to be hyperexcited. I was immediately on my way to Oli's house from where we headed to Piu's place. It was an extremely short notice for us for something as big as a New Year party in The Meltdown. We had to plan and prepare a hell lot of things before nine.

An intense brainstorming session coupled with waxing, home facial, manicure and pedicure began soon to devise a fool-proof plan for our late-night outing.

Piu, the smart one, came up with an idea within minutes.

"We shall say that this programme has been planned and organised by our classmates," she said while scrubbing my face.

"Yeah, it's a good idea. But won't our parents doubt if we don't ask for any money. Any such function asks for student's contribution," Oli said thoughtfully.

"No problem! We will take some five hundred bucks from them and save it for some future expenses," I said, shrugging my shoulders.

"So we need to lie to our parents?" Oli asked.

This girl always became a victim of moral frenzy and she even tried to pull us in. "C'mon Oli!"

She replied, "Okay okay!"

We sealed the deal with our high-fives. Our excitement had increased after devising an impeccable plan for the evening.

9:05 p.m.

The three of us walked towards the main road where Shashank was waiting for us.

Piu and Oli had come to my place at around 7 p.m. with many bags. A lot of preparations had to be done for the supposedly biggest party of our lives. As for me, I had to make extra efforts to catch Shashank's undivided attention. The place would surely be filled with angelic beauties that evening.

Mom had been worried about our safety and I had a hard time convincing her that we would be picked up and dropped by our friends. She agreed, although half-heartedly, only after my promise to remain connected to her at all times.

It was not the first time I had lied to my mother about something, but we were going for a late-night outing for the first time. It made me feel guilty – the feeling that I conveniently chose to ignore.

I was dressed in a pink-coloured knee length dress under a black coat with matching nail paint and lipstick. The bracelet gifted by Shashank swayed down my wrists, along with a couple of other accessories that complemented my dress. It was a cold night, yet we planned to ditch our lowers. We wanted to flaunt ourselves and the chill was not going to stop us that night.

Oli was dressed in a light blue dress and a dark brown jacket while Piu had worn a dark blue short dress coupled with a sexy overcoat. She was looking so hot that she clearly raised the outside temperature by at least ten degrees.

A number of eyes followed us, by the time we neared him. He came out and stood right beside his car, dressed elegantly in a grey suit. He looked damn sexy as usual and I stared at him helplessly until Oli pinched me.

"Good evening sir!" We wished him together.

"Good evening ladies." He saw all of us for a moment and continued, "A lot of guys are going to *melt down* today."

We laughed at his pun.

"Arey seriously! I just thank god that the temperature is low enough for me to keep my stable solid state," he said eyeing me.

Piu said, "Oh please sir! That's an exaggeration unless it's for—"

I interrupted her, sensing the mischief in her voice and advised, "I think we should leave, it's already ten."

"Yes sure!" Piu said and winked at me.

"Please get inside, ladies," Shashank said, signalling my friends towards the rear seat while adjusting his watch.

He opened the front door for me, which made me feel like a queen. I looked at him lovingly as he took the wheels and drove us to the venue.

A silent drive of thirty minutes came to an end as we neared the plush multi storeyed building. He parked the car and waited for us patiently outside as we took a good look at ourselves before stepping out of the car.

Bam! Cold wind slapped my legs and face, the moment I opened the door. Our decision of wearing short dresses appeared to be a total bullshit idea. We walked alongside Shashank, glued to each other, as he showed the passes to a number of uniformed men at the entrance.

I stupidly tried to get some heat from the big curly letters emitting sharp blue light that said 'The Meltdown' with two brightly lit melting ice cubes, the droplets of which reached the ground.

The entire area was decorated with an array of colourfully flickering and eye-catching tiny bulbs. On one of the sides was a giant poster of the singer Mohit Chauhan. It also had Mohit Chauhan's picture and mentioned that he'd be performing live. The mere idea of witnessing a live performance by one of the best singers in India excited us. The night had finally started to get alive.

We entered the building and got awestruck at the huge fifteen-feet-high Christmas tree decorated charmingly with colourful streamers, stars, balls, bells, miniature lights and artificial snow which was staring down at us. It encouraged us to get some snapshots; clicking some pics while our makeups were fresh. Only god knew how we would appear by the end of the night.

Piu took charge as the director immediately while the four of us took turns as actors and photographers.

"Everything good, sir?" I asked him softly while we posed under their direction. He had been unusually silent that night.

"Yup!" He gave me a half-hearted thumbs up.

We got into a big elevator that carried more than fifteen people with us and opened up right in front of the restaurant on the fourteenth floor. The four of us moved in with the crowd and the rapt ambience captivated all of my senses.

The spot was beautifully decorated with white and red satin curtains flowing from one pillar to the other. The glass wall on the exact opposite side showcased the beautifully lit city of Ranchi.

Tables were draped immaculately according to the red and white theme of the night with glasses, cutlery and napkins placed decoratively on them. An aesthetically designed candle stand found its place right at the centre of the table, with a flickering wax light promoting the elegance to the next level.

Someone from the crowd came directly to Shashank and hugged him as we walked through the place. I could not see his face until he turned towards me.

It was Anurag, Shashank's best friend. I knew a few things about him, even though we had never met formally. He looked exactly the same as in his pics. He had a wheatish complexion, although a shade darker than Shashank and was almost as tall.

Shashank turned towards us after a few seconds of boys talk and introduced him, "This is my best friend Anurag and…"

"Anurag, meet Amyra, Priyanka and Olive," he said indicating each of us individually.

Anurag waved at us and said, "Hello ladies!"

"Hello sir!" We waved back.

"Call me Anurag," he said.

"Okay Anurag!" Piu said.

We followed him and reached the table reserved for us. I sat at one side with Shashank, whereas Oli and Piu sat right opposite to us. Anurag sat between Shashank and Oli.

Our table was right beside the glass wall. The town had never looked so exquisitely charming and alive, even though I had spent my whole life there. The beautiful decoration, well-lit toy like houses, the street illuminations with miniature vehicles running on them, the flickering lights of towers, bonfire with people dancing around it and the occasional blitzkrieg emitting numerous colours, added to the scenic splendour of my humble hometown.

Two fine men dressed in black and white with a prominent red bow filled our table with aromatic delicacies that ensured an unstoppable spring in my mouth.

Shashank took the lead, "Shall we?"

Everyone jumped in as if they were waiting for hours for the traffic signal to turn green.

I started with chicken soup along with some non-vegetarian delicacies that were scrumptious.

"When will we see Mohit Chauhan, sir?" I asked Shashank while munching like a cow.

He took out a pass from his coat's pocket and placed it right in front of me and said, "Here's the schedule."

The events for the night were listed in detail on the right side. It would be a long wait before we could get a glimpse of him. Perhaps, a small price to pay.

I suddenly wanted to use the restroom and asked my friends for their company. Oli sprung up like a frog. Piu decided to stay back as we excused ourselves and walked towards the restroom.

Fortunately, I remembered to call mom after we freshened up. We headed back in a couple of minutes to find that Piu had shifted to Oli's place beside Anurag. A smile clenched our lips as Oli took her new place without a word.

A naughty smile clutched our faces while Anurag and Piu continued their one-on-one conversation casually.

The programme was being anchored by a beautiful lady in a red sari, named Kyra, and a handsome man in a black suit, Rajiv. Their deep voices and an immaculate accent charmed everyone.

"So, are you guys ready to get rocked?" Rajiv's voice echoed through the hall after a couple of boring speeches.

"Yes!" Everyone shouted.

"So, ladies and gentlemen, put your hands together for The Rockers!" Their voices turned on the heat.

Everybody was on their feet as the music of the Bollywood song *Kar gayi chull* boomed. The intensity went on another level as they performed two more dance numbers – *Cutie pie* and *High heels.* The jaw-dropping performance was followed by incessant shouts and whistles.

The programme proceeded as per the schedule with beautiful songs, contemporary and hip-hop dances and a mind-boggling performance by The Beatdown.

"Are you ready to dance?" Kyra asked with a flair. The anchors were doing an amazing job of consistently animating the audience.

"Yes, yes, yes!" filled the air.

"Let's rock the floor with the paper dance!" Rajiv said as a couple of men behind him spit out fire.

The floor was soon crammed with fervent participants ready to set the floor on fire. All of us participated in it. I paired up with Shashank, while Piu danced with Anurag. Hilariously, Oli got herself a girl partner, Ruby, from the adjoining table!

The female couple impressed everyone with their spectacular dance moves. We were absolutely stupefied to find Oli sway like that. It was as if a caterpillar had broken out of her cocoon to emerge into a confident butterfly that night. Oli's transformation was breathtaking.

An inexplicable happiness mixed with loads of nervousness crawled into me as I got closer to Shashank. We made it to the last three couples before our nervousness took an edge over us.

Piu did not survive long; but Oli and her partner crushed everyone to become the sensational winners of that night.

It was already eleven when Rajiv announced, "And now, ladies and gentlemen! Please gear yourself up for the main event."

Kyra added, "Please join us to welcome, for the first time in your town, the man with the most soulful voice. The one and only – Mohit Chauhan!" The crowd went nuts as his melodious voice filled the entire place. He came right in the front playing his guitar and singing *Pee loon* from the movie *Once Upon a Time in Mumbai.*

Deafening claps, chants, whistles and standing ovations filled the space as he finished his first song. All that increased manifold as he performed a series of his songs, including some bouncy dance numbers that made us all swing to his beats. I was having the time of my life.

But, I didn't realize that the things that were about to unfold next would change my life forever.

11:45 p.m.

Rajiv shouted over the microphone, "*Aag laga di Mohit sir aapne!*"

"Thank you guys for your love and support. Love you guys!" he said with a big smile and blew kisses on all of us before leaving the stage.

The name chants were finally subdued by Kyra's words that echoed across the place, "Ladies and gentlemen! We will be entering the new year 2017 in a few more minutes, but before that...."

Rajiv continued, "Someone amongst you had requested us for something that no one could have denied, and neither did we."

A sudden silence covered the place with a few murmurs as we looked at them quizzically.

"It's new year time and *love* is in the air!" Kyra turned us into nosey children.

The lights of the place were briefly turned off. Even the candles were blown off.

"Whooooo!" The buzz of an awestruck crowd spiralled as the darkness revealed the several tiny bright stars placed on top of the stage that together formed an, "I LOVE YOU".

"Wow! Who's the lucky one?" My iris protracted as they looked around for the mysterious stranger.

Flash! A bright beam of light fell upon me as my hands reflexively went over my eyes to cover the sudden bright light.

It took me a second before I came out of the bedazzlement and realised that I was in the spotlight.

"What the fuck is going on?" I looked around, but could see nothing but dark figures.

Everyone had shifted away from me. I was confused and wanted to hide.

"This is a mistake!" I uttered.

In a jiffy, another light came on. It took me a few seconds to realise that the second light was focussed on Shashank. I had no idea what was going on!

I trembled nervously and got an urgent need to rush towards the washroom. My hands and legs turned cold as he went down on his knees with a mic in his hand.

Fuck! I knew what he was going to say. I had been eagerly waiting for this magical moment but now I was shaking like a leaf.

"Amyra, I love you!" His voice reverberated in my ears like a nightingale's song.

I felt a sweet thump in my heart and tears rolled down my cheeks. Everyone was mute and my eyes were fixed on one person who mattered the most.

"Say yes!" Someone pulled me out of my trance as the world resurrected.

I hugged him.

"I love you too," my voice resounded through the mic in his hands, announcing my answer to everyone. A series of heart-warming squeals and loud whistles followed my response as my face turned redder than a ripe tomato.

"Congratulations Amyra and Shashank! This calls for a loud round of applause for the hottest couple in town!" Kyra shouted.

"Thank you so much!" We expressed our gratitude when Rajiv jumped in immediately, looking at his watch, "And now, ladies and gentlemen, it's the time that we have been waiting for…"

"Five."

"Four." Kyra caught up with him.

"Three." Every living soul in the room joined the countdown.

"Two."

"Happy New Year!" The place was electrified.

Colourful lights of fireworks spurting right outside the glass wall mirrored on our faces as I kissed his lips. The world became silent for me once again as I reached the stars with him.

"Happy new year, baby!" His lips were locked with mine.

"Same to you baby!" I echoed his sentiments.

When I realised we were in a crowd, I stepped back and he smiled at me. I covered my face with my palms and hurried towards the washroom, followed by my girlfriends. One and all gave way to the VIP's of that evening. Everything seemed unrealistic. It was the perfect beginning of a perfect love story which had an imperfect me with my perfect man! I couldn't have asked for more.

6

Rain Begets Fire

Days passed like hours with Shashank. My world narrowed further and revolved only around him. Piu and Oli seemed to have drifted away. I hardly talked to them, even when they were with me, because I was always busy chatting with the love of my life. The only time we weren't talking was during his classes or while sleeping.

21 February 2017

3:30 p.m.

This was the first day after we had started dating that Shashank had not come to the college.

He was running a fever and wasn't feeling too well. Although it was nothing serious, inexplicable restlessness daunted me. Reluctantly, I had to wait until our classes were done before seeing him, in order to fulfill his request. This was in exchange of his promise to see a doctor.

I was on my way to Shanti Niwas, house number 112, Kanke Road, Ranchi; in the midst of a sudden downpour after attending all my classes. I had to locate a light green-coloured house with a big black and golden gate opposite the electricity department office. It was easy-peasy as the driver knew the exact location. However, the rainfall defence mechanism of the auto rickshaw was not very effective and I was completely drenched by the time I reached.

The gate was unlocked, probably in anticipation. I walked gingerly through running water on an approximately eight-feet-wide red and yellow tiled path that existed amidst a small garden with some beautiful flowers.

I found my shelter in front of the teak door, which stood between me and my love, behind a big portico that had his car parked at the centre.

A loud ding-dong echoed as I pushed the doorbell nervously and retracted my hand back as quickly as possible.

"Hey babe! Did you swim to reach here?"

"Very funny!"

"How are you now? Has the fever gone?" I bombarded him with questions.

"I met the doctor. He gave me an injection and now I feel healthy as a horse." He scanned my curves from top to bottom. "... and you look hot!"

I concealed my smile with pretentious anger and said, "If you are done with your NSP (*nayan sukh prapti*, which was a polite jibe at him checking me out), mister healthy horse, can you get me a towel and allow me inside? It's cold out here."

"Oh okay, sorry!" He went inside hurriedly.

I wringed my dupatta and lower parts of my kurti by the time he came back. I did not want to soil his well-maintained house.

He came out with an absolutely spotless white towel that turned grey the moment it came in contact with my skin. I tried to make myself as dry as possible and stepped in consciously, trying to unsuccessfully stop the water from dripping down.

"Don't worry about that. Nobody's home," he said looking at my worried face.

"Oh!" I said with a sigh of relief and added, "I need to use the washroom."

"This way please," he said and started walking.

I followed him, thoughtlessly making a trail of droplets to reach a shipshape room.

"Can I get another towel?" I asked.

"Of course. I will be back in a minute," he said and went out.

It was definitely Shashank's room. There was a mini library containing hundreds of books that were placed diagonally opposite to the entrance. A double bed was placed horizontally at a distance of few feet in front of the book shelves. A neat study table and chair stood equidistant between the two. The washroom was located right on the opposite side of the bed.

I was busy scanning the room when he entered with another spotless white towel and said, "Here you go, baby!"

"Thank you!" I took the fluffy towel from his hands and rushed into the washroom.

It was filled with vapours as I took a relaxing warm shower. I saw myself in the mirror and wrote on it, "I love you Shashank!" and wiped it off. Craziness overpowered me as I started posing with and without the towels in front of it.

Maybe, the rain had some charming impact which made me lose all my inhibitions. That coupled with some extreme hormonal gushes pushed me to a new level of crazy. I stepped out of the door thoughtlessly with a towel wrapped around my head and the other on my body.

"Fuck!"

Shashank sat on his bed, right in front and gazed at me continually. He must not have expected anything like that.

Under my normal brain functioning situation, I should have run back inside in embarrassment; instead I walked towards him with a lot of passion in my eyes. The concealed embarrassment disappeared the moment I decided to surrender myself to the spell that had engulfed me.

"What?" I grinned getting closer to him.

"Nothing." His eyes were like an innocent child's, but his voice was not. My heartbeat was racing at the notorious thought.

"It's rude to stare!" I said naughtily.

"Sorry!" he said apologetically and started looking at the other side while still trying to get a glance at me secretly.

'He is such a baby! I love him so much!' I thought and said, "Babe, I need to dry my clothes."

"Give it to me, I will put them in the dryer." He tried hard to look only into my eyes.

I was enjoying the moment.

"No!" I exclaimed, "Just tell me where, I'll do it myself." There was no way I wanted him to get his hands on my dirty undergarments.

"Okay," he said and we walked out of the room after I collected my clothes.

We reached another room where all the laundry was kept beside an automatic washing machine.

He opened the door for me and I dropped the clothes in saying, "I need something to wear. I can't move all over your house in wet towels."

"Nobody's going to be home anytime soon," he said mischievously.

"Oh really! Where is aunty?"

"She left for a family function soon after we came back from the hospital, and trust me, she is not going to be back before ten."

"So sad! I won't be able to meet my mother-in-law today." I sighed.

"Very funny," he said sarcastically.

His expression seemed cute to me.

"I am kidding!" I said.

"Oh! I thought you really wanted to meet mom."

The disappointment in his tone made me feel guilty and I said, "Sorry baby. I did not mean that."

"It's okay baby. Even I don't want my mom anywhere near us right now. I am loving to see you like this." He was just playing phoney.

"Huh!" I rolled my eyes and turned my back towards him.

I felt him as he came close to me and said, "I love you!"

"Huh! Stay away from me," I said and moved away from him.

He suddenly hugged me from behind and whispered in my ear, "I want you now."

A ripple of excitement ran throughout as his warm breath hit my ears. Numerous thoughts went through my mind at the spur of the moment. He pushed himself closer to me as I felt his shaft growing against my rear. I had never felt something of that sort before and felt both uneasy and excited. My heart pumped rapidly and I was clueless about what would follow. He turned me around and started kissing me vehemently. I surrendered straight away.

The white turban slipped of as he grabbed a handful of my hair and pulled me closer.

"Ouch!"

A soft 'sorry' was followed by softening of his grip and intense kisses.

Our tongues played with each other as he took me up in his lap and I wrapped my hands and legs around him. I had only dreamt of that moment.

He walked all the way to his room and gently put me on the bed. I was stunned as he unveiled his absolutely chiselled upper body. God! I wanted him all over me!

My wish was granted immediately as he crouched and moved like a tiger to slay me, and I was eagerly waiting to be slayed!

A light push put me down on my back. Eyelids dropped and my body cringed with a mixed sensation of pleasure and tickle as he kissed my neck and ears. I could feel his fully stimulated staff completely dousing my already wet vagina.

'Shit! Am I leaking?' I did not want to pee on him.

"Baby, I want to use the washroom," I said.

"Okay." He stopped

The towel must have gently decided not to become *kebab mein haddi* as I realised that Shashank was on top of a nude me. I blushed and rushed to the bathroom while holding on to my only covering.

A plethora of thoughts crossed my mind in the next few seconds as I sat to relieve myself.

'Was it the right thing to do? What if I was unable to please him? What if my mom came to know about it?'

Eventually, I ignored all of those questions, 'I did not give a fuck to anything. I loved him and wanted to become one with him.'

Strangely, my efforts to pee went in vain. Eventually, I gave up and stepped out to find him sitting on the edge of the bed, facing me.

I took a few steps towards him before dropping the towel. His expression changed and his gaze was fixed on my bare body. The gullible look on his face fetched a victorious smile on mine.

One step more and his breath fluttered through my bust. I put my right foot on the edge of the bed, pushed him down and glided all over him before reaching up to kiss his lips exuberantly for the next few minutes.

He groaned as I slithered down and kissed his body. A strange sensation ran through the veins as my body came in contact with his erect manhood. I moved down and released it.

'So this is how it looks in real!' My jaw dropped as a number of unanswered questions made me scared.

'How the fuck was that thing supposed to get inside me?' The thought scared me.

The eyes refused to look elsewhere and I took it in my hands. My entire body trembled as I kissed it nervously. Manly mumbles of pleasure tendered a supple satisfaction to me.

I got up like a cat and looked straight into his eyes.

Shashank said, "Come over here."

I crawled over to his side where he wanted me like an obedient child. He was soon on top of me on four legs. Our tongues played with each other as he caressed my breast. My eyes closed as I plunged into another dimension.

A pleasingly ticklish feel made me stoop a bit as his lips ran around my neck and shoulder. His maws soon circled my breast as I eagerly waited for it on my nipples. An era elapsed before he ran his tongues on them. I moaned loudly and underwent a quarter of an orgasm already.

He continually sucked them as I climbed up the ladder of pleasure. A momentary pause was followed by his fingers skating in my vagina.

"Ouch!" I yelped at a nimble pain and a sizeable sensuality.

"You are completely wet!" he said, looking straight into my eyes.

The words made me blush and I covered my face with my hands.

"Can't wait to taste you," he said and slid down smoothly through my belly. The assumptions of what was about to follow took me to the next level already.

He put his head between my legs and started licking my clitoris. The room echoed with my moans as he shoved his tongue deeper.

"Babe, I want you inside me! I need you!" I literally pleaded.

He stopped just when I was about to come. How he knew was a mystery to me.

"Taste yourself," he said and kissed me. A faint smell of my fluid filled my nostrils. I soared high into a heavenly world when I mechanically held his erect shaft in my hands and rubbed its crown on my vagina.

Our voices crammed the room.

"Just come in!"

He started pushing the big thing inside me and all my pleasure was replaced by pain.

The words, 'Please stop!' were about to depart my lips when I clogged them and instead said passionately, "Kiss me!"

He came all over me as I focussed my attention on kissing him fervently to make the most of this magical experience. An acute sting was followed by inexplicable numbness as his shaft reached my innermost core. Slow but firm strokes continued and all I felt was sweet pain and detachment. I spread my legs more for him to get further in. His groans increased and so did the intensity of strokes. He was about to come.

He took out his shaft and released into my body with a loud moan. The incomparable look of satisfaction on his face delighted me beyond measure. I was triumphant!

He dropped down and kissed me for a few seconds before plummeting on my side.

"Did you come?" he asked me.

"Nope," I said.

"I hope it wasn't very painful." I could sense concern in his voice.

"A bit. I think that's the way for girls on first encounter."

"Not for my girl!" His words somehow turned me on even in my pain.

"It's okay, I am good. I don't want any more of it." I was actually afraid to do any more of that stuff.

"Just close your eyes, relax and enjoy, babe," he said.

I followed his orders like an obedient student without a word of resistance. I trusted him to not give me any more of the pain and said, "Okay!"

Footsteps around the room ignited my curiosity further as I thought, 'What's he up to?'

The faint sound of the bed and the tension in the mattress announced the ingress of my man.

"Don't open your eyes." A subtle touch of his lips on my ear lobes, followed by a ripple of warm air conveyed the message clearly. He guided me to sit on the bed and blindfolded me with a smooth cloth. A tie, I guessed. The lack of vision suddenly aggravated the hormonal gush in my body.

A gentle push made me lie down on my back and was followed by kisses all over my face.

He then took my hand in his and sucked my fingers one by one. Sensations of pleasure instigated from my fingertips and spiralled through my entire body.

The next moment, he pinched and caressed my right nipple, and licked it by a full stroke of his tongue. I moaned with pleasure, pain was overshadowed by bliss once again. He then lifted my lower back and put a pillow under my butt.

I was thrilled and felt quite vulnerable with the exposure. The feeling multiplied a million times as he stroked me with his tongue down there. I groaned madly as he ran his mouth all over it.

"Don't stop, babe," I almost screamed in bouts of pleasure.

A few seconds passed before I clenched his hair, forced his head in between my thighs and reached my climax with a loud moan.

A heavenly wave of satisfaction ran through my entire body. I removed the pillow from below to relax as he came over to me and kissed my forehead.

He removed the blindfold that allowed a blurred vision, but I preferred them closed. I lay my head on his chest, hugged him and dived into the ocean of love. Silence spoke volumes on our behalf for the next few minutes as we lay still.

"You are the best thing that has ever happened to me," he said.

I sunk further into his arms and said, "I love you."

"I love you too!"

9:05 p.m.

He turned off the engine in front of my house and I kissed him before leaving the car.

That day's events were completely unplanned as I had not told mom anything about being late. Because I did not know it myself. I was very late and her angry face floated around my eyes.

The only thought that overshadowed my mind after dozing off and getting late was, 'What would I say to mom?'

Shashank came up with an idea. He would tell mom that he taught me and wanted me as a co-author in a book that he was writing. For that, he had taken me to the city library where we got stuck because of the heavy rain and bad network. He walked me to the door to face her with me. But to our surprise, the door was locked.

I sighed first and then exclaimed in dread, "Where is she?"

Horrifying thoughts owing to my guilt invaded my mind which made me very anxious. Just then, I heard the voice of my angel once again, "Call her, babe!"

I took out the seldom used key from the innermost pocket of my bag. I unlocked the door hastily and said, "Come in, quick!"

I looked around and told him to follow as quickly as possible. A lot of prying eyes moved around our house, spying on each and every activity. I did not want anything to be reported to my mom.

I gestured at him to sit and dialled mom's number hastily. She was never out for so late. The network was actually very lousy and after five unsuccessful dialling attempts, it finally connected. "The number you are trying to call is switched off!"

"What the fuck!" Beads of sweat sprouted and started dripping from my temple even at that temperature.

I tried again and again but I got the same response. My heart started pounding heavily and my mind was still engaging with the worst possible thoughts.

"Babe… mom…!" I tried to speak, but my voice was stuck in my throat.

"She will be fine. You know the network gives weird messages on rainy days," he said, holding my hand.

"What if she came to know about what I did and thought of punishing me like this?" Even the thought made me shiver. I could not have imagined facing her after that. "I will kill myself if that's the case!" I cried out loud.

"Now please stop talking rubbish, Amy. That seems very unlikely," Shashank said. "Try calling some colleague… or friend… or relative?"

"Yeah!" I started thinking hard and the first name that struck my head was Kunal uncle. I dialled his number but his phone was also switched off.

"What the fuck is happening!" I cried.

"Call someone else."

I made a few other calls to her colleagues and friends, just to find out that nobody had any idea about where mom was. I lost control of myself and switched to intense panic mode. I started breathing heavily and the phone fell from my hands. The world around me started spinning.

"It's all my fault. We shouldn't have done this. God has punished me," I murmured as he saved me from hitting the floor and helped me sit on a chair. I regained my senses within seconds and started crying.

"Babe, I am sure she is fine. She must be stuck somewhere due to the heavy downpour. Don't panic!" he said while hugging me.

"No, nobody knows about her. It has never happened like this. Mom never switches off her phone and it's absolutely impossible that she hasn't called me even once. Something is definitely wrong!"

No words from Shashank seemed to have any effect on me. Ominous thoughts of her meeting with an accident, or suffering a heart attack, or being hurt by a robber scared me to death.

I started praying vehemently. "I am sorry god. Please don't punish me like this. Don't take my mom away from me."

It was the same prayer that I offered, the day I lost my dad. The intense fright gripped me. This disturbing turn of events made me relive the worst day of my life in a moment.

7

I Lost My Dad

10 April 2010

12:30 p.m.

It was a bright and sunny Saturday, brimming with life. I was on the verge of witnessing the thirteenth summer of my life.

Mom was busy in the kitchen while my homework had ensured that my weekends remained jam-packed. Her phone was kept on a table beside me when it started ringing.

It was an unknown number, so I took it to her.

She received and said, "Hello!"

That one phone call changed our lives forever. A seemingly sharp and distressed voice from the other side shook her completely. The phone slipped off her hand and she became unsteady. She managed to balance herself by holding on to the edge of the table.

I ran to her and asked, "What happened mama?"

She did not utter a word and her face lost colour.

I was scared and asked her again and again, "Who was it mama? What happened?"

She tried to compose herself while opening the cupboard hurriedly and said, "Get ready, Amy! We need to get going."

"But where?" I asked.

"Just get ready, Amy!" Mom shouted while changing.

"What happened, mom? Where do we need to go? Is dad okay?" I held her hand tightly and asked her, crying in fear.

She turned towards me and said, "Your dad has met with an accident on the service floor. He has been taken to the hospital. Jai uncle is on his way to take us there."

Mom struggled intensely to stay calm, but drops of tears deceived their way out in front of me. I turned pale and started crying.

"Don't cry, Amy! He will be alright. Nothing will happen to him," my mom assured, hugging me tight.

1:15 p.m.

I stood outside a big white door that read in bold red letters – INTENSIVE CARE UNIT. The letters 'No Entry' on the top stared down at me. An uncle dressed in white sat on a chair blocking the entrance. Nobody could get in without his permission.

Jai uncle had come to pick us up on his scooter. The hospital seemed to have moved miles away from its original location as uncle battled through the busier and shittier-than-ever traffic to reach there. I was sitting in the middle, feeling mom's rapid heartbeat continuously thumping on my ribs.

We were right there when Kunal uncle, my dad's best friend and colleague, came hurriedly with a bag of medicines and handed it over to a nurse who was standing in front of us.

"How is he?" my mom asked him.

"He is unconscious," he replied.

She burst into tears immediately and asked, "Can we see him?"

"I just got a pass. It can supposedly be managed," he said.

"Sir, please let them enter," he said showing the pass to the doorkeeper uncle.

"One person," he said sternly.

Kunal uncle gave the pass to mom and said, "Please go in, sister."

The austere-looking uncle was kind enough to allow me to enter with mom.

We stepped inside and were welcomed by the beeping sound of various machines, a faint sound of oxygen masks and a creepy silence that filled the ambience. A peeving odour made me feel nauseous. My gaze bypassed several patients lying on beds and got stuck at my dad's bed.

I scuttled to match mom's pace as she walked briskly to reach by his bedside. I was shocked at what I saw. A big bandage was wounded around his head where I could still see blood. A number of plugs had been attached to my dad's body. A huge mesh of wires lay all over his body, apart from multiple needles that were inserted here and there. A big pipe that seemed to be pumping oxygen with great pressure and making his body thump was inserted into his mouth, producing a loud wheezing sound. Loud beeps of various machines added to the acute disturbance.

I trembled and started crying vehemently at the appalling sight that scarred me forever.

"Sshh!" The nurse told me to remain quiet and signalled mom to take care of me.

She covered my face and hugged me, but I continued howling.

"Please escort them outside," one of the busy doctors said to a nurse.

"Madam please take her out," the nurse said to my mom.

"Please let us stay here," she pleaded.

"Ma'am, there are other critical patients here. Please try to understand!" The nurse said and pulled us towards the exit.

2:00 p.m.

I was horrified as a nurse opened the door and signalled mom to get in. The doorkeeper uncle stopped me as I held on to mom and started shouting, "I want to go in."

Mom turned towards me and said, "Wait here with Kunal uncle, Amy. I will be right back."

I chose to stand against the wall, a few feet away from the door, and started praying fervently with tear-filled eyes. "Please god, don't take him away from me. I beg you god, please! I won't lie to him ever. I would do whatever he asks me to do. Please don't take him away from me. Please god, please!"

I guess that's what every living soul does in a situation like that, expecting a miracle to happen in our real life. But, alas! Life is not a movie. An intense loud cry made my legs wobble. I knew that voice; it was mom; she had come out.

I ran to her and asked her horrified, "What happened mom?

Mom hugged me tight and cried bitterly, "Amy, Papa has gone far away from us."

I started howling as she pressed my face and embraced me. It was a horrid nightmare that had come true. Memories connected to him came to my mind in a flash. A deep regret for the fights and an inexplicable nostalgia cherishing the merry times with him struck me together.

All my prayers had gone in vain.

8

Thank god, she is fine!

21 February 2017

09:45 p.m.

Bzzzz bzzzz. My phone vibrated flashing mom's name. I took the call immediately and said, "Hello, mom?"

"Yes Amy…" Mom answered from the other side.

The devils playing with my mind were blown away immediately by her sweetest voice.

"Where are you, mom?" I cried over the phone.

"I am at Kunal uncle's home, beta. Your aunty is not well, so I came here to see her."

She must have registered my nasal voice, so she asked, "Why are you crying… all good?"

"Nothing is good. I was so frightened, mom. It's so late and I was unable to get to you. I hate you!"

"So sorry, Amy. Actually my phone got discharged and there was no electricity here. The power supply was reinstated just a few minutes back after which I charged my phone and called you."

"Okay. When will you reach home?"

"Kunal uncle will drop me. I will be there soon."

"Okay mom, come soon. I am waiting for you." It was such a relief talking to her.

I got on my knees, folded my hands and offered my thanksgiving prayer immediately.

I opened my eyes and found Shashank right in front of me. He had joined me, I don't know when. His action was damn cute. I fell more in love with him at that moment.

9

The excursion begins... and so does our naughtiness!

28 June 2017

It was finally the day of our first ever college trip. This five-day excursion to Darjeeling got a green signal by the college management after much efforts.

However, this journey of five days was inclusive of transit time, which meant that there would be just a two-and-a-half-day stay in Darjeeling. The class was not pleased initially, but excitement took over all disappointments in no time.

Shashank had played a pivotal role in getting the job done, apart from our class representatives Shailja and Nikita.

Prof Shashank Raj and Prof Dimple Batra were set to accompany and supervise us. Everyone was delighted to have the company of young professors, especially Shashank. He was the fucking favourite of everyone.

As far as I was concerned, no amount of words were sufficient to describe my feelings.

On the day of travel, we had to board the train from Ranchi station at 8:30 p.m. We reached the station much before time to add to the chaos of the heavily-crowded platform number one.

The typical smell of drains along the tracks, burning iron, electrical sparks, fried and other eatables combined with repulsive odour of everyone's deodorants filled up my nostrils.

A monotonous female voice made announcements, accompanied by beeps and occasionally interrupted by a rough male voice, surpassing the noisy buzz of the passengers.

My eyes worked diligently to find that one person who mattered the most to me. A broad smile featured on my face as my eyes caught the sight of his amazing physique. He looked irresistible in military print three-quarter lowers and a black polo t-shirt.

My face flushed red as he winked at me. I looked away immediately. Damn! That was unexpected in the presence of the whole class.

However, the game was on and there was no way to back out. It was my turn and I blew him a kiss as he joined Prof Batra to mark everyone's attendance. The utter disbelief which was washing over his eyes made me laugh out loud. I continued biting my lips seductively and parading a variety of our love-making gestures secretly as he tried to ignore me while enjoying everything from the corner of his eyes.

He handed over the attendance paper to Prof Batra and sat down on a bench, for a reason that he did not want to make obvious. Neither did I. I was thrilled to have turned him on from a distance.

My thorough enjoyment was interrupted by a nudge from Oli. "She has already called your name thrice."

"Present ma'am."

If looks could kill, I would have been dead that very moment.

"I want everyone's attention right here!" she yelled.

Attendance was reinstated and the brief pause had given him time to relax. He walked a bit away, lost and frightened as I looked up proudly.

Soon, we were all inside the train. More than half of the coach was taken by us. Shashank made us settle on one of the ends, where he also kept his luggage so that he could stay with me all the time. Prof Batra was at the other end with the others.

The moment everyone settled down, the railway coach was echoing with chit-chat, laughter and songs.

Various groups were formed in the compartments, including ours which had Shashank, Oli, Piu, Kiran, Sushmita, Renu and me.

It was only after 1.00 a.m. that everyone's energy tailed off. Only two pairs of eyes seemed immune to sleep.

Shashank was right beside me on my lower berth. He was holding my hand. Silent moments passed by as the sound of the running train was cursorily overpowered by the wheezes. A lot of sensations instigated from our point of contact and glued us further.

He withdrew, got up snappishly and walked away, leaving me with an array of thoughts. He reappeared after a few minutes and signalled me towards himself.

"What? Why?"

"Come here!"

We walked till the end of the coach and various hormones kicked in instantly as my questions found answers.

We kissed and cuddled hungrily for the next few minutes before getting back to our seats and dozing off with dreamy eyes.

A lot more could have happened if our momentary private space had not been that whiffy, but I was happy.

10

Hello Darjeeling!

Mona Inn

7:00 p.m.

We had set foot on the New Jalpaiguri (NJP) station at around two in the afternoon. The climate was hot and humid. The sweat which was trickling down in every part of the body made me overly conscious. Thankfully, the bus for Darjeeling which was arranged by our agent arrived by the time we finished our lunch.

As we ascended the hills crossing a wide expanse of tea gardens, the intoxicating beauty mesmerised everyone. The road was quite scary, with sharp turns, giving me ample reason to hold the man seated beside me. Feeble prayers and mantras befell the ears as the depth of fosse augmented. One side of the road was the mountain that was cut to build the road. It was covered with ferns. The other side were the top edges of the mighty pine trees that had their trunks and roots hundreds of feet below us.

Cute and colourful toy like houses could be visible at some distance as we went higher.

It took around three hours for the bus to reach our destination in Darjeeling. The two of us had caught forty winks, sinking into each other's warmth.

"C'mon girls, move fast!" I heard Prof Batra.

Shashank was still smiling in his sleep, (probably dreaming about me). I nudged him hard. He got up and took over his responsibility immediately.

'How the fuck did he do that?' I wondered.

It seemed rather funny and put a broad smile on my face. The bus stopped right in front of our temporary dwelling place. A cold wind slapped my face as I stepped out of the bus. I could feel the frigid air travelling deep into my lungs and further.

"Mona Inn", it said, in a flashy green and white coloured light that briefly blinded my sleepy eyes.

Mona darling was a two-storey building near a place called 'Chaurasta' or 'The Mall', that's a landmark in Darjeeling. All sorts of public events like the musical concerts, dance shows, rallies and *dharnas* take place right there.

Google *baba* told us everything beforehand.

The people of the place seemed to be larks. It was just seven and they were winding up their shops already.

'No night strolls.' I thought.

We were welcomed inside the hotel by a beautiful traditional stole and a desirable cup of hot aromatic Darjeeling tea.

The reception area was noisily crammed by us for the next thirty minutes until the formalities of check-in were completed. Two occupants were allotted a room each. Oli and I had got room number 302 whereas Piu and Varsha were assigned the adjoining room 301.

In the hotel room

8:00 p.m.

The tap ran continuously, trying to cover up Oli's out-of-tune voice as she took her long shower.

My phone beeped and it was his message, *Hey babe.*

Hi!

What's up?

Missing you! What about you? I typed.

Just entered my room, he replied.

Which floor?

Third.

Wow, which room? I asked excitedly.

303. Just beside you babe. I couldn't help staying away from you. He pinged

Muaaah! I sent some kisses.

Muaaah! I got some right back.

TTYL babe.

Okay. I knew he was busy.

I love you! he signed off.

I love you too!

I scurried towards a towel-clad Oli, who had just surfaced out of the washroom and kissed her cheeks in excitement.

"Eeeeee!" She was puzzled and pushed me away, trying to ensure her only covering did not fall apart.

"What the fuck! Control your emotions, Amy," she shouted, "You used to be straight. Call Shashank!"

"Shut up!" I said trying to shush her. "He is in next room."

"Thank god! My dignity is safe," she said with a fabricated sigh.

"Don't be so sure!" I caught the edge of her towel and said with a cunning smile.

"Sorry... sorry... please leave me!" She enacted, pleading with folded hands.

We started playing the scene of Duhshasana disrobing Draupadi, as depicted in the *Mahabharata*.

She prayed, "Lord Krishna, help me!"

"This is *kalyug*... No one's gonna..." I was just saying when the doorbell psyched us up.

"C'mon now, she did not need saving yaa," I said looking upwards, at heaven perhaps.

"OMG, your intention was this bad!" Oli guffawed. "Who is it?" She shouted out loud.

"It's us."

I opened the door after recognising the voices of Piu and Varsha. It was already time for us to go to the restaurant for dinner.

"Hey guys! Did we interrupt something?" Piu said mischievously looking at Oli.

"Thank god you dropped in! You guys are my saviours," Oli continued, "This monster tried to rip apart my dignity!"

"How dare you, Amy?" Piu said. "We cannot allow you to have all the fun alone. Haha!"

They joined me and all of us walked towards Oli, as she ran back to the washroom and shouted, "Fuck you bitches!"

Golden Oak Restaurant

8:30 p.m.

It was a simple, no-frills restaurant with rectangular tables and four chairs around it.

It was a buffet and we walked sluggishly towards the counter, chit-chatting loud enough amongst ourselves to outdo the clamour that resonated. My eyes occasionally (although the occasion recurred every few seconds) looked towards the entry gate for Shashank who had disappeared after our extremely small chat.

Our dinner was over by nine and there was still no sign of him. He had not even seen my texts. All of it raised my anxiety.

We were all set to leave the place when a loud clap by someone attracted our attention. It was followed by the voice that I desperately wanted to hear all this time.

"Students, may I have your attention please!"

The loud noise dropped to a mild buzz, followed by complete silence as Shashank's voice reached everyone. That was his power over all the students!

He entered the restaurant with Prof Batra, our travel agent, another person dressed in a black suit, probably the manager of the hotel and a few papers in his hand.

I got my answers as to where he might have been.

He started, "I have the schedule for tomorrow in my hand."

"We will head to Tiger Hill first thing tomorrow morning, to see the world famous sunrise. It will be followed by seven or eight other sights before we come back to our rooms. The bus shall be here at three, so ensure that you are ready before its arrival."

The murmurs began as soon as we heard 3 a.m.

"Silence!" Prof Batra shouted at the top of her voice.

Shashank continued, "You heard me right girls, get ready by three tomorrow morning. It will take us nearly one-and-a-half hour to reach Tiger Hill. That said, I suggest you get into your beds early so that you are ready for tomorrow."

The agent whispered something into his ears and he continued, "And yes, we shall be back by two in the afternoon."

We all nodded, and he confirmed, "Any questions?"

"No sir!" The answer was unanimous.

"Okay then, finish your dinner and get a good night's sleep everyone," he said and turned around to leave.

"Good night, sir!" everyone shouted.

He smiled, saw me with the corner of his eyes and left the place with them.

"That sounds fucking hectic! Let's get some sleep," Oli said as we walked out of the restaurant.

"Yeah—!"

I was mischievously interrupted by Oli, "You wanna sleep, baby?"

"Of course, she wants to sleep with...." There was no way Piu would have let go of this opportunity.

I immediately jumped into action and pulled Varsha forcefully to get away from them, "Let's distance ourselves from these losers!"

They laughed outrageously at my words as we sped towards the room.

Waiting for him!

10:00 p.m.

Oli was already snoring while I tossed in bed. It was already ten and Shashank was nowhere to be seen. I had checked my phone more than a hundred times to ensure network connectivity.

My WhatsApp chat screen showed a single tick for the message that I had sent him from the restaurant at 8:38 p.m.

I was unable to control myself and typed in, *Where are you babe?*

And the message got delivered.

Hey babe. Just came back to the room.

Was busy preparing for tomorrow.

Sorry!

I love you!

His messages jumped in one by one. But I had got the much awaited opportunity to showcase my anger.

Huh, I don't wanna talk to you. How can you just forget me like this?

Nobody can forget to breathe... you are my life... he typed. *I love you.*

His words melted me like butter on a hot pan, but I wanted to linger it a bit more.

No... you liar. I garnished my message with a few tearful emojis.

Sorry sweetheart... I really love you. The message was followed by a dozen of emojis and gifs showing his apology, love, kisses, hugs and much more.

Finally I typed, *I love you too.*

He sent in the dancing emoji that literally made me laugh. A moment later, the amusement transmuted to some amatory feelings, creating tingling sensations in my body.

A part of me wanted to just get into his arms and make love throughout the night. However, the 'sensible me' knew that stepping into his room at this hour with girls in the adjoining rooms still awake was a terrible idea.

I wanna kiss you. He spoke my mind.

Me too.

Come to my room. Just what I had been wanting to hear, though unsure.

Now?

My phone rang in response and I picked it up in a split second.

"Hello! Are you serious?"

"Yup, come to my room," he sounded absolutely confident.

The sensible me was thoroughly kicked by the stupid and hopelessly romantic me as I landed right into his lap, kissing him ravenously.

In no time, he was all over me. We made love as unobtrusively as would have been possible. Rest of it was taken care of by the television.

It was the quickest one ever, not lasting more than fifteen minutes.

We did not even talk much and I was back in my room to find Oli smiling in her sleep. My body felt completely relaxed and all I wanted was to sleep in his arms (which was not possible then.)

We chatted for the next few minutes before I dozed off with the phone still in my hand.

11

Kinky start… Now where is he lost?

Tiger Hill

30 June 2017, 4:30 a.m.

We reached Tiger Hill at around 4:15 a.m. and were shocked to find all the good sight-seeing points already taken by other tourists.

The three of us somehow managed to get our asses on a big cold rock. I felt the chill running through my spine to the top of my head in addition to the one that cut through all my warm coverings and pierced my bones from all sides.

The hostile wind slapped my cheeks red. Piu literally glued herself to me from the right side while she had Oli on the other. She enjoyed the warmth while the two of us took the wrath of winds upon us.

An announcement in the most wearisome voice informed us that sunrise would begin at 4:57 a.m. with medium-to-low visibility due to the fog.

That was a bit disheartening, but there was nothing anyone could do about it.

All I wanted at that moment was to enjoy the stunning sunrise with Shashank. I looked around and the familiar voice struck my ears, "Looking for me?"

A broad smile stretched across my face and I said, "No."

He had been standing behind me from a long time.

Piu showcased her presence of mind by pushing Oli, "Shift fatso…"

The three of us shifted to make not-so-sufficient space for him. He sat to my left so I tried to get hold of his right hand. He clasped my hand in his far left hand and my waist with his right hand.

Wow! His hand seemed quite warm even at that temperature and gave me a warm fuzzy feeling. He found his way under my clothes and started rubbing my waist and tummy. Cold wind also found its way in, but I chose to focus on enjoying his touch.

"Stop it! Someone may see," I whispered in his ears while trying to shake off the ticklish feel.

"Not so lucky, gal! No one can see us," he answered mischievously.

I looked around. He had a valid point. Visibility was low, the rock behind concealed us and there was no one on our side.

A subtle consent from me encouraged him further, and he played thoroughly with my body. His fingers found its way under my bra as he rubbed my nipple to an extent that made me wet.

"I can hear your moans now. Save it for later." That was Piu talking shit.

"I wasn't moaning, bitch!" I whispered in her ears.

"Did you want me to wait for that moment?" she asked.

"He can hear you. Stop embarrassing him!" I said.

"Okay okay," she said apologetically.

She looked at him and he smiled back. "No probs!"

"See! All good," she said.

The scenic ambience of the partially-visible mountainous terrain, large coniferous trees, beautiful birds and their melodious chirps was suddenly overwhelmed by the buzz of hundreds of people within a few minutes.

Everybody ran to and fro to grab the place for the best possible view, whereas we stood at our place, trying to get rid of dust in our clothes (while I was busy tidying my clothes stealthily).

Oli caught the sight of Shashank who was waving at us from the top of a rock after our brief cleansing session and she rushed to defeat any other competitor from our class. We followed her victoriously until the finish line.

In a couple of minutes, god splashed the sky orange and the adjoining Mount Kanchenjunga in its colour. This mesmerising display of beauty lasted for just a few seconds and we were fortunate enough not to miss it.

Most of the girls recorded the entire show in their mobiles and cameras, whereas Shashank and I captured this magnificent scene through our eyes. Pictures and videos can never truly replicate the beauty as experienced by a human mind.

However, we did click a lot of pictures. A number of tea vendors moved across the place. It would have been rude not to have a cup of steaming black tea at the Tiger Hill top in Darjeeling at around five degree centigrade.

Soon, our bus raced towards our next destination. It had been a magical start and we hoped the day to be the same.

Back to our Room

4:30 p.m.

I was sitting in my room looking at the pics that we had clicked. Oli too was busy with her phone.

We were back at the hotel by four. Lunch had been pre-ordered and prepared in the hotel itself. All of us were famished after a tiring yet thrilling day and literally rushed to the restaurant as soon as we hopped down the bus.

I scrolled down my screen looking at the pics and reached the page where Shashank and I had dressed ourselves in traditional Nepali attire in the Batasia Loop. We looked great together and my mind went ahead in time, creating our wedding fantasies.

The dresses, the jewelleries, the preparations, the makeup, the rituals, the vows, the excitement the happy faces, the parties, the singing and dancing – all created a splendid mental picture that overwhelmed my mind, body and soul. I could not wait to walk down the aisle with my man and say 'I do'.

Everything seemed perfect.

I dozed off with my beautiful thoughts until the uncanny doorbell woke me up.

Oli was dating the perfect man in her dream. The smile revealed it all. The devil in me wanted to kick her, but my angelic self chose to let go.

I got off the bed and opened the door while rubbing my eyes.

"What's up with you guys? Not even answering your phones!" Piu's voice quickly cleared the cobwebs in my head and eyes.

"Get up, sleepy head!" she shouted at Oli.

Smack! Oli got a tight spank on her butt as she tried to turn around and sleep.

"I was just getting to fuck him yaa! I curse you to face the same situation," Oli said irritated.

"As if I am gonna wait that long!" Piu winked and smacked her again.

"Ouch! God is never going to forgive you for doing this to me," Oli said, getting up.

"I am okay with that. Now get ready quickly," Piu said.

"Why? I don't want to go anywhere," Oli replied.

"Stop being a wimp, Oli. This is the first day of our tour and you people are just hell bent on wasting time sleeping," Piu complained.

She had a point.

I was ready by the time Oli moved her lazy arse from the bed to the washroom.

The advantage of cold weather is that you don't have to worry much about your clothes, but I had to worry about my makeup because my man was right there, surrounded by a bunch of charming bitches and I did not want him to take his eyes off me.

Piu decorated my eyes, lips and hair by the time Oli got ready.

"My god! Someone's gonna fall again today," Oli said looking at me.

I blushed as Oli put a small black mark from the eyeliner behind my left ear, "May all the evil eyes glance off."

Shopping @ Chowrasta

6:00 p.m.

We purchased some stuff from the local market in Chowrasta and immediately kept the change in our purse after we got ourselves some handcrafted souvenirs.

The trip had just started and we were already running out of cash.

However, we were soon tempted by the amazing aroma of local delicacies in the market. There were a number of stalls lined up, offering a variety of dishes.

We stopped in front of a stall called Thapa's. A very handsome north-eastern guy, who became Oli's crush instantly, came to our service.

He made us sit on plastic stools and gave us a small menu card which had an assortment of over fifty items. Varieties of chowmein, momos, typho, thukpa, chicken phale and the list went on.

"We should start with chicken momo" Piu was in no mood to waste any time.

"…and then we will have thukpa," Oli continued.

"...and then typho and chicken phale," I jumped, my mouth already watering.

"Phale will require at least twenty minutes, madam!" the young man said in a typical Nepali accent.

"Bring us two plates of chicken momos first, and also start preparing two plates of chicken phale," Piu placed the order.

"Okay madam," he said and went off quickly.

Oli continued looking at him from the corner of her eyes as he got busy with other customers.

"*Jiju* found! Free local delicacies of Darjeeling arranged for," I said playfully.

She nudged me as the two of us winked at her.

"He is so handsome!" Oli said dramatically.

The two of them started talking about him, whereas I tried calling Shashank for the fourteenth time since we had left our room. All my makeup and stuff would be a sheer waste if he did not see me.

'Where the hell was he?' I contemplated helplessly.

That feeling of being unable to get in touch with him, even after being so near was highly irritating.

"The number you are trying to reach is out of network area. Please try again later," the lady announced in my ears again and again.

I disconnected the call and put the phone into my purse indignantly.

"He must have got busy with something. After all, he is a faculty member and has a lot of responsibilities." Oli's words hardly had any effect on me because he had never acted like that before.

'Is he with some other girl?'

'What if he is tired of me?'

'Maybe he is looking for options!'

While my mind was restlessly engaging with these depressing possibilities, it was immediately overshadowed with guilt at my creepiness.

'You better get involved with your friends, Amy!' I thought and started talking to them. Soon, twelve pieces of steaming hot momos, with soup and sauce were placed on the plastic stool in front of us. I treated myself with its exotic taste coupled with exclusive girl talk for the next thirty minutes.

Hotel room

09:15 p.m.

That was the first time I had a heated conversation with Shashank. Actually I was the one speaking. The moment we stepped into the hotel, I was extremely irritated to find him busy entertaining all the girls of our class except us. All my efforts and makeup to impress him seemed to have gone in vain.

I ignored him completely and walked to our room. I spoke to him angrily when he came to cheer me up. He apologised repeatedly, but I wasn't ready to hear anything from him. He finally gave up and left, the moment I questioned his character and loyalty.

I cried endlessly for the next few minutes – firstly because of my anger, jealousy and Shashank's betrayal. Secondly, because of guilt and shame for all the things I'd said to him. I wanted to talk to him, but was too embarrassed. Finally, I fought through all those negative thoughts and switched on my phone to give him a call. He had apologized a hundred times to me; it was my turn.

One hundred and eighty-three unread messages with apologies, love emojis, kisses and hugs made me feel incredibly special. I was speechless. I was not sure if any other person would have put that much effort that Shashank did after what all I had said.

I replied immediately, *I love you too.*

My phone rang the moment he saw my text.

"Hey babe, I am sorry!" His voice choked.

"It's okay baby! I over reacted. I am sorry!" I had tears in my eyes.

"Don't be, honey. I love you!" he said lovingly.

"I love you too." My words carried sincere emotions.

"Can you come to me?" he asked.

"Now? Isn't it too early?" I said, presuming his intentions.

"I know, and I don't care!" he replied.

We could still hear girls moving around outside in the alley.

The girls inside room 302 understood my dilemma and signalled me to agree with him.

"Okay, I will be there," I said at the support of my friends and disconnected the call.

I looked at Piu curiously and she said, "We will get you to him and leave soon after wards. Understood, dumb-ass?"

"Yes," I replied gleefully.

Shashank's Room

9:45 p.m.

The girls got up to leave the room and said, "Bye sir!"

"Bye, girls!" Shashank said.

Piu winked and made me blush as the two of them left to give us the much-needed privacy.

"I am sorry!" I started talking.

"No… no… baby, I am sorry," he replied.

The rhythm of his voice had transcended from being apologetic to intensely sensual since evening.

"I love…"

He did not even allow me to complete my sentence. Within few minutes his tongue was inside, brushing every corner of my mouth. We were in the bed within seconds with him on top of me.

The fucking doorbell made us stutter.

"Who is it?" Shashank asked out loud.

"Dinner sir!" A timid voice came through the door.

"Just a moment!" The irritation of an unwanted disturbance could be seen on his face and I enjoyed it. His restlessness for my closeness was making me feel more special.

"Okay, sir," the voice seemed to have turned softer.

"I had told the receptionist to send it to the room around ten while entering the hotel and completely forgot about it," he said while still on top of me.

"Go and get your dinner, sir!" I smiled, pushed him and walked towards the washroom.

I rolled my eyes at him as he opened the door.

He looked at me with folded hands as I locked myself in. The waiter took nearly four minutes to keep the stuff and left the room.

I came out when Shashank knocked to find one heck of a dinner decorated on the table. Five chapattis, a bowl of rice and dal, mutton curry, salad, vegetable fry and papad.

"Are you really gonna eat all of this by yourself?" I asked.

"Yes, I am famished," he replied.

He always had a big appetite which seemed to have grown in Darjeeling.

"So Mr Dinosaur, complete your dinner."

"Nope, this dinosaur has now been served with its favourite food. He will eat that first!"

"I am no food, Mr Sha…!"

Déjà vu! He had already pinned me by the wall before I could finish my sentence.

Something was unusually distinct. It was the first time that we had a serious fight. He had been guilty and so had I. Then, when things got resolved, we were categorically starving for each other. We craved for passionate intimacy and cruised into our world of love within seconds.

He removed my top and I undressed him while continually kissing each other. He had just unhooked my bra when the doorbell rang again.

"What the fuck?" Shashank uttered.

I was fucking irritated and my head was drowned in the thought, "Screwed for the second time in a matter of few minutes. Maybe it wasn't our time!"

"Who is it?" he called out loud.

"It's Piu, please open the door, sir!"

That was odd.

He got into his shirt and leapt up to open the door immediately. I followed him while wearing my top. Oli and Piu forced themselves into the room without a word.

"What's wrong?" There was a lot of nervousness in my voice.

"Girls from other rooms are planning to meet sir now."

Shashank looked at Piu with disbelief and said, "Meet me now, why?"

"Varsha told me about it. It has something to do with going to Gangtok on their own," she replied.

"That's not possible," Shashank replied.

The doorbell announced the arrival of the most undesirable guests of the moment.

Oli opened the door, "Hi!"

"Oh hi…! Did not expect to see you here," Puja said as she entered the room with Varsha, Archana, Megha and Dipti.

"Oh! The whole gang is here." We waved at each other.

"Good evening sir!" they said.

"Good evening, girls, please make yourselves comfortable!" Shashank said in his usual gentle tone.

His hospitality added fuel to the fire of my annoyance.

'Why the hell did he have to be that decent!' I thought and made faces at them while they were busy finding suitable places to sit.

"Sorry to disturb you in the midst of your dinner," Megha opened the conversation while sitting next to the table filled with eatables.

'You *should* be sorry for what you did, morons,' my thought was evident enough to be understood by Piu and Oli because they signalled me to cool down.

"It's perfectly fine. My dinner arrived just before Amy and the group came to me," Shashank replied.

'Again such kindness. Tell them to fuck off!' I could feel my head heating up.

"Actually sir, we wanted to know if we could head towards Gangtok on our own on 2 July?" Megha said.

"You want to go to Gangtok when all others return to Ranchi?" Shashank acted surprised.

"Yes sir," they answered collectively.

"I am sorry girls, but I can't allow that. It's my responsibility to get you people back to Ranchi safely," he rejected their request right away.

"Please sir," they pleaded.

"I am sorry girls. But I cannot allow that!" he said adamantly.

A wave of satisfaction brought a smile on my face as I heard them plead while he constantly repudiated.

"Okay!" They said dolefully after realising that their proposal had been invariably turned down.

"Please reconsider it sir," Dipti said in the sweetest ever baby tone we had heard till then. She did not leave a stone unturned.

"Don't be hopeful ladies," Shashank said plainly.

"Sorry to disturb you at this time sir," Megha said.

"No problem," he replied.

'I have a big problem. You guys just ruined our moment and mood.' The compelling thought forced me to make faces at their back once again as they left the place without even wishing him good night.

"I don't understand the reason of them coming to talk about something that could have easily waited until tomorrow morning," Oli said.

She was right. Something was fishy. Maybe, the girls had seen me entering his room alone. Maybe, they knew about us. Maybe they were extremely jealous of me dating him. Maybe, they wanted to catch me red-handed with Shashank. I didn't give a fuck.

"You should go to your room, girls," Shashank said after a while.

"Yeah!" My voice was utterly distraught.

"We are waiting outside for you," Oli whispered in my ears and they left the room.

We kissed for a few seconds and I went off to the room all wet!

12

The Super Rockstar!

The Rock Show

1 July 2017

The last day was quite boring and did not offer much besides some local sightseeing and shopping. We paid some formal visits for pics to the Rock Garden and some tea gardens in and around the vicinity of the town after our brunch.

The major attraction of the day was the rock show in the evening. We were looking forward to seeing really hot northeastern guys performing right in front of us.

It was soon time and almost all the girls of our class were present in the party lawn – an open space on one of the sides of the hotel. The three of us took our spot near the three-feet tall barricade that distanced us nearly ten feet from the stage.

Most of our classmates had remarkably decked up eyes, glowy, fair skin with blushed rosy cheeks and had perfectly lined lips that evening.

'Gosh! I had to protect my man from all of them.' The thought turned me restless and I started looking for him all around. Instead, I caught the sight of Sonal, the tomboy of our class, who never came out of her usual denims and shirts. But today, she had put on a fabulous knee-length maroon dress, black jeggings and high heels for the evening. The short hair revealed her matching danglers and a necklace. She looked stunning.

I admired her for a minute and resumed at 'Mission Shashank' to find everyone else, but him. He did not even answer my calls and I hated that all the time. God knows where he disappeared every so often.

The programme was scheduled to begin at six. A local band named Clefs and Breaks was invited to perform and everyone was fired up to sway to the beats of some hot guys.

Unable to find Shashank anywhere, I shifted my attention to chatting with my friends.

"Good evening, ladies and gentlemen!" We looked towards the stage. "I, Shraddha, welcome you all to *the rock show*."

The pleasing voice pulled everyone's attention. All the eyes were fixed on the winsome girl, clad in a red short dress, which was exhibiting her attractive legs. She held a silver microphone and walked towards the centre of the stage.

We have always been jealous of northeastern girls for their immaculate hair and spotless skin that never seemed to tan or age. Shraddha epitomized that kind of timeless beauty. She continued speaking while I was glued to her looks. Her deep eyes, her perfect face that flaunted every feature sharply and her elegant nose was mesmerizing. My eyes looked away when she gave way for the welcome speech by a middle-aged gentleman and went backstage.

He was the chairman of the hotel and delivered the shortest speech ever heard by us.

"Thank you, sir!" Shraddha took back the mic and continued, "… and now ladies and gentlemen, it's time for the rock show to begin. Please join your hands together for *Clefs and Breaks*."

All of us started to clap and cheer as six guys dressed in cool casuals occupied the stage. Three of them took the guitars, one stood behind the synthesizer, one took charge of the drums, while the sixth guy – who seemed to be the lead vocalist – took the centre stage. He was Rehan and he introduced the band to us.

"Is anyone out there?" I felt his bold voice right around my liver.

"Yeahhh..." All the girls shouted.

He shouted at the top of his voice again, "Is anyone out there?"

We replied back with same energy, "Yeeesssss..."

"Nice to find a bunch of young, energetic and beautiful ladies out there! Men, no offence meant!"

His statement was followed by a loud chuckle.

"Are you ready for some bad ass rock music?" Rehan shouted.

"Yeah!"

"Are you ready to let the music get into your nerves!"

"Yeah!"

He spilled out tremendous amount of energy on us. "Yeah... then let the head-banging begin...!"

The show started with the song 'Crawling' by the Linkin Park and was followed by five more heavy metal songs.

Jumps and head bangs had already made us sweaty.

"Are you fucking tired?" he said breathlessly.

"Nooo..." We shouted.

"You better not, because it's time for a special performance from someone amongst you! So... hold your breath and welcome..."

He chuckled, "I won't say the name, you'll know!"

The whole place started buzzing as we looked at one another, wondering about that *someone amongst us.*

My phone vibrated with a beep and I checked my phone immediately. It was him, *Just for you, babe!*

'What's for me?' I was still thinking about it when the music started and a very familiar voice filled the whole place, "*You are my fire. The one desire*!"

It was Shashank in blue denims, black t-shirt and a leather jacket. The whole place was on fire as the girls saw their favourite teacher, all set to perform for them (but nobody knew it was for me). Everyone was psyched as he performed the song 'I want it that way' by the Backstreet Boys, which was followed by a rock number 'Numb' by Linkin Park.

I saw him performing live for the first time and I must admit, he nailed it. We were enthralled to discover the colossal energy levels, charisma and impeccable panache that took the head banging and ground thumping to the next level. The whole place was covered with smokes of dust.

"Shashank sir... Shashank sir..."

Rehan said on his mic, "Shashank sir! I must say, that was soooooo hooooooot!"

"Once more, once more, once more..."

Shashank replied, "Thanks a lot everyone," he turned towards the band members, "And thank you guys, you are awesome musicians. Wish you the very best for future!"

"Thank you so much and hats off to you sir," Rehan said.

The hoots and his name-chants did not stop long after his song was over.

I pinged him. *I love you Mr Shashank Raj.*

I love you too. I got the reply quickly.

Where are you?

On your left.

I turned and saw him darting straight towards me. However, the girls clung to the rockstar, brimming with excitement, hugging, applauding and taking selfies with him.

Shashank's efforts to tear through them to reach me were obvious, and I was extremely jealous. I wanted him to be around me *only*, to hug him, kiss him; but that did not happen. What I got was a long distance conversation through our eyes. Was it sufficient for me? Hell no!

We bumped into each other momentarily in the midst of his fans. I saw right through him and went off for dinner with my friends. The feeling of envy and anger overpowered me once again.

13

Drifting Apart

I had been with him for more than eleven months now but things still seemed as fresh and exciting as the first day; until we came back from Darjeeling. We had shared the best moments of our life-going out on dates, group hangouts with friends and moving around painting the town red. I was mesmerized each time he sang.

His poems were so romantic that it made me feel that I was the luckiest girl in the world. Every time he dedicated a verse to me, I fell for him more. We created better memories every day; those that would emphatically bring smiles whenever we looked back.

However, things had turned out to be quite different between us in the last three-and-a-half months. It seemed that we had drifted away from each other, creating a vacuum, especially after our Darjeeling trip. This was mostly because of our semester examinations.

His expectations had driven me into full study mode. My mind had idolised him, not only as a husband, but also as an inspiring mentor. I wanted to make myself worthy of him. One of the ways I planned to do was, by outperforming everyone else in the class, like he had done during his college days. That was the least I could have done to match up to him. I did not want him to be ashamed of me. So, I ensured that studying became my new hobby.

In my conquest, I forgot the fundamental rule of maintaining a healthy relationship – communication. We did not meet and hardly talked over phone. We just exchanged glances during his periods and some academic-related conversations in between our classes. That's it! Moreover, he had become much more popular after the excursion and was surrounded by girls all the time. That deteriorated things further – firstly, because of my extreme jealousy coupled with insecurity; secondly, due to my self-generated inferiority complex that was pushing me further into study mode; and thirdly, because of those fucking whackers who were hovering around Shashank and ate up any valuable minutes that I could have had with him.

Twenty to thirty minutes a day (which reduced exponentially with time) had become the maximum time for our interaction, which was absolutely nothing as compared to those limitless hours we had spent over the phone till a few days back. Guilt overtook me each time I spoke to him over ten minutes. Although, he tried to support me by not forcing me into long conversations or to meet after college, an uninvited void emanated in our relationship. This led to stupid fights every day, which reduced our conversations even further. Although things got sorted easily, I had started feeling a drastic change in his attitude towards me in the last few days. Maybe he had gotten used to staying without me. I knew it was my fault, but I was confident that things would get better after the exams ended.

But, I was wrong. Things turned miserable after that. This time, it was he who did not have time for me which led to more conflicts than ever. I did not feel special like before and he said he felt the same way. There were no more poems, no more songs, no romantic talks. It felt like the beginning of the end.

However, as I had always said, "God favoured our relationship!" It was a déjà vu and he gave me a big opportunity to make things right between us, on his birthday.

14

Perfection matured by a year

20 September 2017

I had been saving my pocket money for the last few months to buy something decent for him, but the task at hand was absolutely perplexing. There are a hundred affordable gift options for a girl, but when it comes to guys, we hardly find a thing.

After discussing with Piu and Oli, we zeroed down to presenting him with a shirt. We hopped through a number of multi-brand showrooms before buying a beautiful bluish grey shirt and a card from Archie's a day before.

It was his first birthday with me and I wanted it to be etched in our hearts forever; just like he had done for me. I knew that I may not be able to match up to his standard. But I was determined to do whatever it took to mend things and make them brighter than before.

I called him thirty minutes before the clock struck twelve to ensure nobody wished him before me. I had to defeat a long list of bitches, witches, fuckers, whackers and vipers (that's an exhaustive list of slangs, I know). Basically, my rivals who would to steal my man. I knew they were lined up to get to him first, but not on my watch.

He received the call after a few rings and said, "Hello!"

"Hello baby, what's up?" I asked lovingly.

"Nothing as such. I was just going through some journals. What about you?" he said.

"I was just sitting and thinking about you," I replied smilingly.

"*Achcha*... and may I know what my baby was thinking about me?" he asked curiously.

It was after days that he had addressed me as 'my baby' and I felt so special.

"It's just that, I love you very much!" I said, stressing on every single word.

"I love you too honey!" he said affectionately.

The endearment gave me wings and I was on cloud nine. I could already feel a change in the air.

Our chit chat continued as I looked at the time on my phone – 11:59:43.

Silence prevailed for the next few seconds as the clock struck twelve and I started singing, "Happy birthday to you... Happy birthday to you... Happy birthday, my dear baby... Happy birthday to you!"

"Thank you so much," he replied and I continued, "God bless you in abundance and give you all the happiness and success, and everything you wish for, my love!"

"Thanks a lot sweetheart. But all I wish for is you," he replied.

I was overjoyed upon hearing that. Now, it was my turn to make him feel the same. He was special, always, only I was stupid enough to not make him feel so in the last few days. Well! I think that's how stupid people like me learn, after making mistakes.

This was followed by a long conversation after which we dozed off. The next morning started with an hour-long conversation, during which he invited me and my friends for lunch at Hotel Lark.

In preparing for it, I had attempted to write a small poem for him, which I decided to pen down with shimmering ink on the left side of the card.

Hotel Lark
20 September 2017

12:30 p.m.

We bunked our classes that day and reached the venue in the afternoon. This was the first time that Shashank did not have a problem with us bunking those absolutely boring classes.

We were standing right outside the posh building of Hotel Lark. I called him and he took the call immediately, "Hello!"

"Hey, birthday boy! Where are you?"

"I am in the restaurant. Where are you guys?"

"We are just outside the hotel."

"Okay, I will be there in a minute," he said and hung up.

We walked through the portico and stepped into a huge air-conditioned space to find a big reception desk occupied by finely dressed girls at the front right corner. A mini lounge area, set up with luxurious leather sofas and a glass table, was placed few feet away from the reception. We decided to enjoy the view until he arrived.

I was busy appreciating the interior when someone blindfolded me from behind. It did not take me even a second to recognise the touch. I got on my toes and hugged him tight.

"Happy birthday, my love!" I whispered in his ears.

"Thanks a lot, honey!"

That moment was spoiled by the intervention of my very jealous friends who uninvitedly barged it. We weren't even done.

"Happy birthday, sir!" They said loud enough for all eyes to turn towards us.

"Thank you, ladies," he replied.

"This is for you, sir," they said and handed him the colourful bouquet made up of a variety of beautiful flowers.

After a brief photo session, Oli took the bouquet from his hands and giggled. "We will take care of the bouquet, sir. You should hold on to your property."

"Okay! May I?" Shashank smiled and asked for my hand in the gentlest way.

I put my palms on his as he led the way. "This way to the restaurant."

He put his hands around my waist as we walked and whispered, "You look ravishing!"

I was dying to hear those words from him. It was my right after hours of heavy labour.

"Just for you." I blushed as those words came out of my lips.

"Thank you so much," he said and casually kissed my ear, giving me goosebumps immediately.

Piu and Oli were five to six steps ahead of us, to give us the required space.

"Just a sec!" he said and stopped abruptly.

He took a few steps back, leaving me in bewilderment and said, "I did not get a chance to look at you properly."

I smiled as he scanned me from top to bottom and I flaunted myself. His eyes spoke volumes.

'Mission accomplished!' I thought and a victorious smile clenched my lips. My eyes got fixed on him.

A trouser in the shade of blue, a light pink shirt with a waistcoat, a blackish-brown leather belt, a pair of awesome shoes, a new watch (mom's gift) flashing on his wrist, his impeccable personality and everything super-garnished with an alluring spark in his eyes.

He looked super hot. I was dazed.

"I wanna eat you, right now!" His whisper brought me back from my reverie and kicked butterflies in my tummy.

"I am all yours. Have a bit of patience," I said biting my lips seductively.

"I love you!" he said in a voice imbued with inexplicable passion.

Man! He was turning me on.

"I love you too!" I said and continued, "Babe, can we afford some private time elsewhere, after lunch?"

"Why?" He had a naughty flash in his eyes as he asked.

"I have a surprise for you," I replied with a wink.

"No problem! That can be managed," he said confidently.

I brushed his cheeks with my fingers and said, "It better happen, birthday boy."

"You are driving me crazy. Should we leave already?" he said impatiently.

I smacked his arm and said seductively, "Have some patience."

He threw out a long heavy breath and said disappointedly, "Okay! God, please give me the strength!"

I couldn't help but laugh at his reaction when the *kebab ki haddis* retrieved their steps and Piu said impishly, "Guys, this is a public place. We have cameras all around."

We soon reached a beautiful teak finish door on top of which was written, 'Palaash Taste of Jharkhand'. It was guarded by a fairly dressed gatekeeper cladded in a grey-coloured uniform, white gloves, a large turban of maroon and grey along with a matching scarf on his neck and waist. That neat guy greeted and promptly opened the door for us.

The interior was absolutely different from the exterior of the place. It was a fully tribal themed multi-cuisine restaurant. I had never seen anything like that ever.

The place was dimly lit with yellow bulbs installed in kerosene lanterns. The light ignited nostalgia as I travelled back to my early school days when we faced regular power cuts in the evenings.

The walls had illustrations of tribal people engaged in various activities such as dancing, merrymaking, marriage, farming, hunting, etc. Most strikingly, the tables were an exact replica of big kettle drums that were surrounded by four cushioned bamboo chairs and a couple of stools imitating a *mandar* (a kind of tabor). Water jugs and glasses of copper were kept on every table, in addition to a small hookah, as seen in villages. Wall hangings were made out of sickles, spears, bows and arrows. I wasn't sure if they were for real.

The ambience had taken me back to my granddad's place, my favourite childhood holiday destination.

I was in my trance which broke when a fourth voice hit my ears.

"Hey girls!" It was Anurag waving at us.

He was trying to place candles decoratively on the beautiful round-shaped cake. It was festooned exquisitely with chocolate chips and wafer sticks. On the centre were embossed the words, 'Happy B'Day Shashank' with white cream.

"Hi!" we replied in chorus and I took charge of the candles immediately.

He seemed more than happy to get rid of the work and grinned, "All of you look fantastic."

The choir repeated, "Thank you!"

Anurag used the hookah like a microphone and announced while rubbing his tummy, "Let the party begin. I am starving."

"Okay! You verified *bhukha-nanga*!" Shashank said sarcastically, making us laugh out loud.

In a couple of minutes, he blew out the candles and cut the cake neatly, putting the first piece into my mouth. I took a small bite and put the rest in his as everyone else clicked our pics.

"Happy birthday!" I handed him the card I had written and the box that was wrapped securely, so that he didn't bother unpacking it in front of my eyes.

"Thanks a lot!" he said.

Soon, he took out the card after treating everyone else with the cake and started reading it as I got busy eyeballing. It did not take him long before he caught me checking on him. His eyes glistened and he blew a soft kiss. I looked by my sides and sent a flying kiss back.

"C'mon! We know about you guys. Don't try to hide it from us." Oli poked me.

I replied, "Shut up! We are not hiding anything from you. It's the people around us."

"Did you write it yourself?" Shashank asked looking at me.

"Yes, I know it's not as good—" I replied apologetically.

"It's awesome, babe. I never knew you had such great writing skill," he said lovingly.

"C'mon, you are exaggerating!" I blushed.

"Nope, it's absolutely amazing. I am speechless. Thanks a lot!" he said and kissed my hand.

His words gave me positive vibes as I replied, "Welcome sweetheart! It's only for you."

"I love you, Amyra."

"I love you too," I replied happily.

Suddenly, Piu snatched the card from Shashank's hand and I yelled, "Piu! Don't, please!" I tried to get up and take it back from her, but Shashank held me back.

She started reading it out loud as I closed my eyes and ears to prevent the embarrassment that awaited me:

I wish you happy birthday, my love!
You're the first thing in my mind as the sun knocks my ingress,
The moon sings a lullaby of your name as my eyes get heavy in the darkness.
I wish you happy birthday, my sweetheart!
You are the reason of my happiness and smile,
The best thing that ever happened to me since I was a child.
I wish you happy birthday, my babe!
You transformed from my want to dire necessity in no time,
You, the perfect creation has been unjustly burdened with carrying the overly flawed ass, that's mine.
I wish you happy birthday, my sweetheart!
There are no words to express how much I love you,
I pray that god bestows all the success, happiness and good luck on you.
Lots of love, hugs and kisses
Amyra

"Wow!" Oli and Anurag exclaimed collectively as Shashank looked incessantly into my eyes.

20 September 2017

4.30 p.m.

I was staring at a duplex bungalow in Morabadi, one of the plush areas in Ranchi, after a forty-five-minute ride followed by an amazing lip-smacking and finger-licking session.

"Whose house is it?" I asked.

"You will know soon enough," he replied with a mysterious smile.

Shashank acted annoyingly secretive at times. Although I loved his surprises, but that day had to be my turn.

We had bid goodbye to the others and Anurag had agreed to drop Oli and Piu home, so that we could have some private time.

Shashank took a road that led away from his house after leaving the restaurant, which meant we were not going there. Of course! His mother was home.

I watched the road as he drove intensely. We did not talk much, none of us wanted to.

We finally reached a house which I was seeing for the first time after a silent drive. He parked the car along the pathway and I stepped out of the car as he walked towards the doorway. The next moment, I saw him taking out a key from his pocket and unlocking the door of that house.

"God! You have the keys. Whose house is it?" I asked again.

"Wait and watch, honey," he replied.

I stepped in after him to find a lavish living room inside. The drawing-cum-dining hall was furnished with leather sofas, oak wood furniture, fifty-two-inch TV with a home theatre system, lush curtains, light fixtures and antiques. The whole interior of the house was professionally designed.

Immediately, I caught sight of a sizeable photo frame incorporating three people. One was Anurag and the other two must be his parents.

The guy seemed filthy rich.

"He has a lot of money!" I exclaimed.

"Yup, a self-made man," he replied proudly.

"They are his parents, right?" I asked pointing towards the frame.

"Absolutely," he said.

"Do both of them work?" I inquired.

"Our fathers were *chaddi buddies* and even he is a retired banker. Aunty is a homemaker and an excellent cook," he informed me.

"Okay, so your friendship is the family tradition." I winked and we smiled at each other.

"And what do you mean by self-made?" My curiosity was snowballing.

"Well, he is an interior designer who has made quite a name for himself. His client base is spread across India and even abroad," he replied.

"Wow! I did not know that," I said appreciatively.

"Hmm… anything else?" Shashank said sarcastically. He wasn't interested in my questions so I changed the topic right away and asked, "You sure, nobody would jump in anytime soon?"

"Yes, uncle and aunty are out of town. They won't be back until next week," he said.

"Neighbours?" It was a rather stupid question, but I had to clear all my doubts.

He looked into my eyes and said with a smile, "People in this neighbourhood don't have time, honey."

"Okay!" I said.

"Any more questions?" he asked.

"Just one more," I said mischievously.

"Proceed." He sighed.

"Where?" I winked and he pointed towards the staircase saying excitedly, "Upstairs."

15

Zero Void

We landed in a big room with a queen size bed in the centre.

"Is this where he sleeps every day?" I was startled as I uttered those words.

"Nope, this is the guest room."

"Okay," I said while trying to look at one of the biggest rooms I had ever seen. However, Shashank was in no mood for any further talks. He pounced on me like a hungry lion and started kissing me vehemently.

I loved to find him hungry for me all the time, and this time, it was after a pretty long gap.

He caressed me all over and mashed my lips. He pushed his tongue past my clenched teeth to reach mine. His stubble scraped against my cheeks. His hands were on the verge of undressing me when I held them just in the nick of time and pushed him away and said, "Easy tiger, there is something special for you."

I smiled as he looked at me like an innocent child who had been stripped of a lollipop while he was about to put it into his mouth.

I went to the bathroom and dropped the dress to reveal my black-coloured two-piece lingerie. The reflection in the mirror made me feel like an erotic dancer. It seemed funny but I was aroused by looking at myself. I stepped out of the bathroom to find him sitting, just where I had left him.

His eyes seemed to have bugged out and glued to my body, giving me a feel of intense hypnotic power over him.

"How's the surprise?" I said, showing off myself sensually.

"Awe… some!" He had never stammered until then and continued, "I want you, *now*." The last word was overstressed and extensively prolonged.

"Ssshhh!" I put my index finger on his lips and signalled him to sit back.

He recoiled silently as I unbuttoned his shirt and pushed him down, right under me. I turned on some soft sensual music in my phone and started showing some recently practised moves to put up a show for him while slowly getting rid of my lingerie.

"You make a move and your balls shall pay the price," I said in a bold and dominant voice.

"Okay!" His submissive tone was an absolute turn on for me.

I growled near his lips and kissed all around his neck and ears before going down to lick and play with his nipples. He sank further into the bed and puffed out a heavy breath with a hum. His hardened shaft pleaded for freedom from inside his trousers and I wasted no further time to grant its request. The unleashed beast was then in my hand and I played with it for a jiffy before rolling my tongue all over it. I pressed the crown between my lips and sucked it hard as he groaned in pleasure. He tried to rise up and get hold of my hair.

"Nope," I said and bit the side of his thigh as a punishment.

"Ouch!" He carped and threw himself back to his position.

"Good boy!" I smirked and put all of him in my mouth. I started stroking and brushing it on the inside of my cheeks as heavy moans found their way from my ears to my heart, rendering my head to swell in pride.

A long rigorous blow job session accompanied with intensified groans was followed by a brief silence as I crawled upwards rubbing my bust against his, until my breasts dangled on top his face.

"Open up!" I said.

My highly obedient babe acted accordingly and I lowered my nipples into his mouth. It was then my turn to moan as he sucked them. The sensations spiralling from those two points rendered me completely wet. I slipped downwards to be right on top of his shaft.

"God, I wanted to feel it so bad!"

Our groans resonated heavily in the room as I rubbed the crown in my clitoris.

"Wow, wow, wow!" The words came out of my lips helplessly.

A brief pause to those moments of ultimate pleasure for me was *de rigueur* as I had to take him miles before reaching my climax (which was just on the verge).

I moved down for the second time and presented him with another transitory blow job.

"Where is the condom?" I asked him.

"Left pocket," he sounded drunk.

"I am going to put it for you today," I said, looking into his eyes.

"You're the boss!" he said subserviently.

I took it out from the pouch and a mouth-watering chocolaty fragrance filled my nostrils.

The next moment, I got on top of him and guided the shaft inside a completely wet me. It slid inside instantly and made me quiver momentarily. The position seemed awkward until I got attuned to the penetration and started riding him. Pleasure coupled with the thrill of hearing Shashank moan made me forget my pain promptly.

I put my palms on his chest while rubbing and plucking both his nipples to intensify his pleasure. A feeling of exhaustion and breathlessness started taking over me after some time of riding. I slowed down, wanting him to take the reins.

Not a word came out from my mouth, but he pulled me towards himself, hugged me and started thrusting me hard from below. This sudden attack made me drown in sensuality. I did not want to boss him anymore and gave in completely.

"Yes baby, fuck me harder." Those words came out tactlessly as he gave numerous big jolts before coming on top of me and doing it even harder.

The sound of him hitting me crammed the area as I spread my legs further and he got deeper and rougher. I moaned stridently and clasped him with all my limbs while he opened his mouth and sighed raucously as we reached our climax.

"I love you." I said while breathing heavily.

"I love you too." He kissed me and took his place right beside me.

I loved his act after making love.

"Happy birthday, baby!" I wished him after getting back my breath.

"Thank you for such a beautiful and erotic gift, sweetheart," he replied.

"Did you like it?" I asked.

"What do you mean? I am euphoric," he said.

A triumphant smile spread across my lips that was instantly kissed followed by an affectionate hug. We lay there quietly for several minutes with my head on his chest, listening to his rhythmic heartbeat. I had no idea when I dozed off.

"What's the time baby?" I tried to open my eyes lazily and asked him.

He got out of his sleep and reached for his phone, "It's six twenty two!"

"Fuck! I need to leave immediately." A sudden surge of energy originating from an unknown source propelled me to get on my feet in a jiffy and get ready while Shashank rolled on the bed lethargically.

"Please get up. I am already late," I said.

"It's my birthday and I never said I was done!" he looked at me mischievously.

"God, you sound so lascivious," I said with a smile.

I got into my dress and tried to pull him up. The opposite happened as he pulled me down on himself and whispered in my ears, "Who said I wasn't!"

"Uff!" I was saying when he interrupted me with a fake superficial smile and said, "And I am your *pati parmeshwar*, right?"

"Oh yes! My personal god, please let me go now. I promise to worship you to the fullest the next time," I said, folding my hands playfully.

"*Tathastu!*" He enacted blessing me with his open palm and got up to get ready.

16

End of (College) Days

13 January 2018

It was the last internal assessment exam. Which meant an informal end of graduation classes. After that day, we would visit college either for clarifying our doubts or for matters related to final examinations.

Oli and Piu were already at my home as you might expect, flipping the pages of their notes while I stuffed myself with chapattis and paneer curry that Oli's mom had sent for me. My mom had left for Hazaribagh the previous night to attend the marriage of a distant cousin. So, the onus of my tummy had been handed to Oli's mom for a day.

Both the girls were busy stressing and preparing with full force while I had somehow developed the happy-go-lucky attitude for this exam and just waited for it to get over long before it started. I did not even care about my performance. It seemed to be mostly because of the distance that had developed between us during my last exams. Shashank would have killed me if he came to know about my thought process. However, he wouldn't know; so I was safe.

The last ten days had felt like a decade. All I got was a glimpse of him while he was busy taking classes. He wasn't even assigned as an invigilator for us, or maybe he denied it deliberately to avoid causing me any distraction. But it was soon going to be the end of all the impediments and then, there was nothing that would stop me from talking, chatting, moving around and having fun with him, at least for the next few days before our final semester examinations.

Was it really gonna be so?

13 January 2018

Noon

We stood at the balcony outside our examination hall on the fourth floor, staring at the campus that had been our home for the last three years.

The square, where all the performances were held, the ground where we sat and spent hours giggling, the college canteen where everyone enjoyed lovely conversations over a cup of tea, the basketball court where the students moved around in groups, and above all, our department.

A strong sense of nostalgia engulfed my mind as memories flowed relentlessly as we walked towards Shashank's chamber.

Oli knocked, "May we come in, sir?"

"Yes, come in!" The voice meant I was going to see him after a long time.

We stepped in and bumped straight into Maddy, Reshmi, Parijat and Jaya

Reshmi was talking to Shashank about the day's paper while Maddy asked me, "Hey, how was your paper?"

"It was okey-dokey types! Yours?" I asked back.

"Just average," she replied dolefully and I knew she was lying.

This was the general answer to such questions after exams irrespective of how someone had actually fared. The truth was always exposed later, through results.

"Thank you, sir!" Reshmi's discussion with Shashank was over in the next few seconds.

All of us hugged and wished each other before they left the room. It was a special feeling that day. The differences and insecurities of the past years were already buried in the past. It was time to move on.

"Good afternoon, sir!" we wished.

I was compelled to address him as *sir* as we were in the college premises. But, all of that was about to change very soon. Time was about to offer me the liberty to baptise him unapologetically as per my desire.

"There is something I needed to ask you girls," he said after a brief discussion about our paper. His voice brought me back from the world of doting pet names. "Is there any chance that I can have all of you at my place tonight for a party?"

"As in *a night-out*?" Oli needed clarification.

"Yes,' he said.

Nobody expected that, especially Piu and Oli, and they looked at one another in bewilderment while I had the answer on my fingertip, because my mom was out of town.

"Okay! I will be there," I said excitedly.

"You ought to be there Amy, the question was for your friends," he said with a smile.

Both our parents were out of town that night. Fate had generously offered us a golden opportunity to spend some quality time with each other (that was what I thought then). He was not going to let the opportunity go; neither was I.

He sensed their anxiety and said, "Don't be so worried, girls! You can discuss and plan out the stuff as per your convenience. I definitely hope to see these charming faces in my house this evening."

"Are you sure, our being there is the right call?" Piu had her own set of doubts.

"Of course, even Anurag shall be stopping by tonight," he tried to clarify.

"Okay, it's cool then!" Her expression changed from apprehensive to elated the moment she heard that name.

Although Piu had never accepted it openly, her eyes had a remarkable spark whenever she heard Anurag's name. All of us, except her, were certain that she had pretty strong feelings for him. They would have been paired up, if he wasn't already dating Payal.

"I will inform Amy, sir!" Oli said hesitantly.

"Okay, no problem. Take all the time you have until evening." Shashank chuckled.

17

Into the storm

13 January 2018

6:00 p.m.

The biggest hurdle for the evening's plan were our parents. We had to give them a pretty solid reason to be able to enjoy the party whole-heartedly. After an intense deliberation, Piu came up with an excellent suggestion, "Well, we could say that it is Varsha's birthday and she wanted us to stay with her for the night!"

Our family was well aware of the latest addition in our friend's group after the Darjeeling trip. Although she preferred to hang out with her group, there were occasions when she joined us to hit small restaurants or visit places. Her friends were cool about it, so there had been no problems.

Things worked out pretty well for me. I was home alone, and my mom did not mind me staying at Varsha's place on her birthday, if Oli and Piu were with me. She was already burdened with the guilt of enjoying herself at the marriage function while her poor daughter was all by herself, struggling in life.

Even Piu did not face any considerable resistance from her family. But, we got calls from each other's mothers to confirm the authenticity of the plan.

However, things did not work out that smoothly for Oli. Her father was adamant and rejected her request of staying out all night. Fortunately, she managed to get permission to stay at least for dinner with strict instructions to be home by nine.

"Were we wrong that day?" I questioned myself.

'Yes and No!' I got my answer looking at the mirror.

Yes, because cheating on parents can never be justified; but c'mon! Who doesn't do that? Every human being (barring some exceptions) has been dishonest to their parents at some phase of their lives.

And no, because we couldn't be harsh on ourselves. We had the right to live life to the fullest, to love and be loved. We deserve that. So, in a nutshell; it wasn't a big deal.

Oli had reached my place by 5:30 p.m. while I was busy getting myself into my red kurti and white leggings. She was dressed in a pink kurti and yellow leggings. We had pre-decided to dress ourselves in Indian attire because our families knew that Varsha's parents were quite orthodox.

She had just completed my eye makeup when someone knocked at the door. "It must be Piu, I will open the door," Oli said and went out.

"Okay!" I replied, while still giving the final touch. It had to be perfect in all ways. I was going to be with him after a long time. I was admiring myself in the mirror when a second image appeared behind me in the mirror. It was Piu.

I turned around in disbelief, "Are you kidding me?"

She had put on a peach-coloured knee length dress and a black cardigan.

"There was no electricity in my home. This was the only decent dress available for me to wear," she tried to explain.

"I hope you don't catch a cold," Oli said worriedly.

"C'mon, it's longer than the dresses we wore on New Year's Eve!" she replied sarcastically.

Oli and I looked at each another. There was nothing that could have been done then; hence, we decided to ignore her action, even thought it seemed quite obnoxious.

So, there we were in the cab after a few minutes. Piu had taken the front seat, whereas we reclined at the back, talking and giggling. Oli and I had covered ourselves with grey and white cardigans, respectively, apart from our stoles.

We did not forget to carry a small bag which contained a set of clothes to keep ourselves comfortable at night. I had even packed an extra pair of top and shorts for Oli, just in case.

Piu was inexplicably quiet through out the drive that evening.

"Is everything okay?" I asked her.

"Yeah, why?" she turned around and asked.

"You seem different today. If it's about your dress, you ought to know that we are cool about it," I replied.

Oli supported me with a short formal buzz, "Hmm!"

We were not okay with it, but we had to pretend at that moment.

"No! I am good. Just don't feel like talking," she said straightforwardly.

"Okay!" I replied, confused. Things seemed odd, but we had to take her word for it. What else could we do!

"Slow down, *bhaiya*. Take right... stop!" The driver applied the brakes at Piu's instructions and the car came to a halt smoothly, right in front of Shashank's house.

"How much?" I asked.

It was a text message from the cab service provider.

"One hundred and ninety eight, madam," the driver confirmed the amount that had appeared in my message.

Piu took out two hundred bucks from her purse and gave it to the driver.

I got down with a heavy breath while staring at my future house. I was expecting myself to be blown away, weaving thrilling fantasies about my future with Shashank but something felt weird. My heart was filled with a sense of anxiety, something I was unable to comprehend.

We entered through the huge black iron gate and reached the door. Piu was about to reach for the doorbell when Shashank opened the door and smiled. He must have seen us entering the premises.

I smiled looking at his chiselled physique that was temptingly obvious through the off-white polo t-shirt and dark blue track pants.

"Welcome, girls! Pleased to see you all," he greeted us in the doorway.

"Hello sir! Thank you," Piu and Oli responded together.

Unprecedentedly, he stepped forward and hugged me and whispered, "I love you!"

"I love you too!" I replied.

He then turned towards them, "You people look beautiful."

"Thank you, sir." They replied in chorus again.

"No need to call me sir," he said.

"Okay *jiju*!" Piu said with a chuckle.

"That's a big promotion. I like that." Shashank high-fived with them as I blushed.

"Well, the person for whom you've dressed so sexily will join us shortly!" He winked at Piu and it was then our turn to high-five.

"I did not get ready for anyone. It's for me, me and only me!" She rolled her eyes as we tittered continuously.

"Get in ladies! I have a lot of space to sit and talk comfortably." He said, while leading us into his spick and span house.

"Make yourself at home, girls. No formalities, please. Everything is at your disposal. If you need something you can't find, I am right here."

"Okay jiju!" The *saalis* said lovingly again. Shashank was totally flattered and there was no reason for him to not be.

Oli and Piu sat on one sofa while I chose to sit beside my man on the sofa kept opposite to theirs.

"Would you like to have some tea or coffee?" he asked. The sexy man of the house was ready to get at our service.

"I think we shall like to have tea," I said with an oomph.

"Uff! Anything for you ma'am," he said, fanning himself with his fingers.

"Get a room, guys!" Piu spoke something of her own accord for the first time that evening.

"Things have not gone that out of hand, Priyanka!" Shashank winked. "Just give me five minutes," he said and stepped towards the kitchen.

"What was that? Were you trying to offend him?" I asked.

"He is very cool. I don't think he would mind his sister-in-law pulling his leg!" She tried to defend herself.

I rolled my eyes.

Oli interrupted before I could have said anything further, "Guys, cool down! This is no time to fight."

She looked at Piu and signalled her.

"Okay, I am sorry!" she said putting her hands up in the air.

"It's okay!" The words came out of me instinctively. But everything was not okay. I felt it in my bones.

"Our jiju is so sweet!" Oli tried to pacify.

"A real man; I want a person like him," Piu jumped in instantly.

"Shashank and Anurag are similar in many ways." There was no way I was going to be left behind.

"Not again guys; he is taken!" she said with folded hands. "I am not going to be the girl who breaks his relationship."

Her voice was serious, which made me feel guilty.

"Sorry!" I said apologetically.

"Yeah, I didn't mean anything either." Oli held her hand and continued, "Sorry!"

The awkward silence was broken by Piu, "It's okay, bitches! I knew you didn't mean a thing," she said slyly and started laughing hysterically. "Look at your faces!" Her laugh didn't stop. She was playing us.

"Fuck you, bitch!" I said and showed both my middle fingers to her.

Oli took a moment to realise and said, "Witch, you got me worried!" and nudged her.

"Aaah!" She whined while still laughing and said, "I felt that hard, you asshole!"

"What did I miss?" Shashank was back with four cups of tea on a tray and placed it on the table.

"Nothing jiju, we were just messing with each other," Piu said while passing the cups to everyone.

"Hmm, interesting!" he said thoughtfully.

"It's perfect!" Oli took a sip and smacked her lips.

"Thanks dear!"

"Superb jiju. This is one of the best I have ever tasted."

"C'mon, that's not true, Priyanka," he said modestly.

"No, really. You have exceeded our expectation," she continued.

"What does that mean?"

"It means that Amy has been praising your cooking skills; especially the tea that you make." Oli continued, "So, we decided to trouble you."

"It was no trouble at all; and all of this is really flattering." The man tried to hide his face from us.

"You know you are blushing, jiju!" Piu teased him.

"Don't bother him!" I came to his rescue.

"Anu will be here any moment. He called while I was in the kitchen." He changed the topic immediately. His words shifted the focus towards Piu as we all looked at her in a jiffy.

"What?" she exclaimed.

"Ding dong." She was answered by the doorbell.

"Here he comes! Someone prayed vehemently." Shashank smirked.

"Hey ladies!" Anurag said radiantly as he got near us and placed two large bags on the table in front of us.

He was dressed in camel-coloured chinos and green-striped polo tee. Piu was unable to get her eyes off him from the moment he entered.

"Hi Anurag!"

"What's up?"

"Nothing, just messing with each other!" I said, looking into Piu's eye with a triumphant smile.

"And, you missed a wonderful cup of tea prepared by our loving jiju," Oli said affectionately.

"*Jeee-joo!* That's interesting!" Anurag sneered and looked at Shashank.

"I have saved tea for you." Shashank got up quickly.

"Don't bother, bro. Sit down!" he said with a smile.

"Okay then, let's see what we have in here," Shashank said and decked the whole table with the items that came out of the carry bags.

We were left awestruck to find two bottles of scotch, a bottle of vodka, three bottles of beer, french fries, nachos, a plate of mutton and vegetable kebab each, two plates of chicken drumsticks, a plate of paneer and vegetable chilly, two plates of fish fries, three plates of stuffed *kulcha*, rice bowls, three plates of chicken curry, dal tadka, salad, at least a dozen sweets, disposable plates and glasses.

"Isn't this too much for us?" I said while looking at my girlfriends. They nodded their heads in approval while still trying to believe their eyes.

"Don't worry girls, we have one heck of an appetite." Shashank came to his bestie's rescue.

"But you are not going to drink too much, or I'll personally drain all of it," I said in a rigid tone.

"Okay *bhabhi!*" Anurag's address made me blush immediately.

"Bhaaaaabhiii!" Oli and Piu repeated the word, deliberately stretching it to annoy me.

I swept aside their banter and started taking out snacks for everyone to munch as they continued to pull my leg. Shashank joined me while Anurag began preparing the drinks.

"I won't drink," Oli said.

"Why?" Anurag asked.

"She has to go back home," Piu answered.

"Oh! A drink won't hurt," he said and poured one for her.

"My father would kill me if he came to know about it," Oli said worriedly.

"Nobody here would tell him, right?" he said looking around at every one of us.

"I know, but my mouth would stink." She had her own set of logical apprehensions.

"Oh! This will take care of that." Anurag opened the bottle of vodka and made a drink for her.

"Are you sure?" she asked doubtfully.

"Yes! Your mouth wouldn't smell. That's for sure." Shashank reassured.

"Okay!" she said and joined us in the toast hesitantly.

"To our graduation!" Piu shouted.

"And our friendship!" It was Anurag.

"And our love!" I said.

We raised our glasses in the air, shouted "Cheers!" and took our first sip.

From then on, we ate, drank and chatted, losing all sense of time.

"Hey Oli, what's wrong?" Piu's loud and considerate voice startled us.

All eyes turned towards Olive. She was near tears. "I have to go home. My father will kill me if I reach late." Her speech was dull and slurred.

I picked up my phone immediately to check the time; it was fifteen minutes past eight.

"We have a lot of time, Oli," Piu tried to console her.

Meanwhile, Shashank asked Anurag, "How many drinks did she have?"

"Just one!" he answered and they exchanged a bewildered look.

"No, I won't make it in time. Do come to my funeral guys." She burst into tears and continued, "I am still a virgin. I don't want to die like this, Amy!" Unexpectedly, she got up and hugged me.

Still confused, I tapped her back and comforted her. "Nothing's going to happen, babe. We will ensure that you reach home on time." All of us tried to control our laughter as she continued to drop tears.

"Don't worry Olive, I am a driving maestro." Anurag tried to comfort our one-drink-high innocent friend.

Shashank brought a glass of lemonade from the kitchen. Piu took out some dishes from the packets in a plate for her to eat before leaving. She cried continuously and ate only a few spoons of rice and a small piece of kulcha reluctantly.

The watch said twenty minutes to nine when Anurag got up and said, "Okay Olive, let's get you home."

She got up, left everything and walked towards the door the moment she heard that.

"I'll join you. She is in no condition to tell you the way to her house. Moreover, I don't want to be the weed among roses!" Piu said naughtily.

"Yes sure, let's give the love birds some private space and time," Anurag added.

"Take her to some pani puri stall and make her drink some of that *khatta imli paani*," Shashank told Anurag while ignoring his comment.

"Okay bro, and we will take a long ride if you want us to." Anurag started the car and teased us.

"Drop her and come back soon. We have to finish our party," he replied.

"Okay, bye!"

"Bye Oli!"

"Bye!" Her voice revealed that she was still high.

Shahank burst into laughter as soon as they left.

"Shut up! I am worried for her and just hope she feels better by the time she reaches home!" I said, looking angrily at Shashank.

"Okay, sorry! But how could she get high on one drink?"

"She isn't a drunkard like you guys, huh!" I pretended getting angry and walked away from him.

Shashank followed me all the way inside the living room, hugged me from behind and said, "You think you can outrun me, babe?"

He loosened his grip as I turned around and said, "Who the hell wants to run?"

He lifted me up by my waist and I wrapped my legs around him. The sounds of our kisses echoed along the hallway as he carried me to his bedroom and closed the door behind us.

13 January 2018

11.00 p.m.

I was fucking exhausted and had dozed off after two continuous rounds when a soft voice echoed in my head, "Hey, sleepy head! Get dressed. They will be home any moment."

Shashank was on top of me as I rubbed my eyes and asked with a long yawn, "How long did I sleep?"

"Fifteen minutes, may be," he said.

"Okay, and where are the two?" I asked suspiciously.

"They had gone towards the highway for a drive and one of the tyres got punctured," he replied.

"I hope they are fine." I was worried.

"They are good. You go and freshen up," he said.

Time passed swiftly as Shashank lay on the sofa with his head on my lap. I was playing with his hair as I told him about my relative in Hazaribagh where mom had gone to attend the wedding function.

"We could have easily gone for another round!" he said naughtily.

"Your bad luck babe!" I joshed.

He got up, pushed me down in a split second and put his hands inside my top, poking and caressing my torso. "Bad luck? I will turn it into my good luck right now."

I gave in immediately when the sudden honk of the car interrupted us.

"Fuck you, Anu!" he murmured as he got up.

"Do you really want to leave this and fuck him?" I flaunted my body seductively.

"You are driving me crazy. Let's keep the door unlocked and get to the room," he said heavily.

"Stop it, you despo!" I nudged him.

"Ding dong." The doorbell announced the arrival of the Anurag and Piu.

"Here they come! Now go, get the door. We have the entire night for ourselves and I have lots for you," I said sensually.

18

Hangover

14 January 2018

6:00 a.m.

An intense headache, burning eyes, parched throat and body pain welcomed me that morning. I felt like shit and looked around in bewilderment. It took me a minute to realise where I was. I looked around; Shashank was nowhere to be seen.

"Where are you, baby?" My voice was languid.

He was nowhere to be seen. My body failed me as I attempted to get up to look for him.

"Hellooo... are you there?"

Nothing again. I tried with all my might and successfully pulled myself out of bed.

"Baby?" I looked in the washroom. There wasn't a soul in the room, except me. I checked the clock that said five minutes past six.

'Where the hell is he?' The perturbing thought dominated my mind as I walked into the kitchen and drank three glasses of water at a single stretch for the first time in my life. Hydration rekindled my fucked up brain, 'The fitness freak must have gone out for his workout.'

I walked in the living room massaging my head continuously and kicked a glass of water on the floor, spreading the water all around. A chicken bone floated along with it.

"Shit!" The place was a complete mess. Bits and pieces of eatables lay all across the room in the wrappers, plates, floor, table and sofa, apart from empty scotch and water bottles that were thrown here and there. I was deeply embarrassed to have been a part of that last night.

'Don't worry Amy, you will unmess it!' Self-doubt crept in immediately as I convinced myself and looked around.

Thump! I tried to sit softly on the sofa, but landed uncontrollably, trying hard to recollect last night's incidents. Slowly, I began to recollect last night events.

Shashank and I had waited impatiently for Anurag and Piu in the living room as they were busy getting freshened up. Anurag showed up after ten minutes while Piu took much longer.

"Are we really gonna do this now, guys?" I looked at Shashank, while Piu sat next to Anurag on the other sofa as he prepared drinks for all.

"Of course!" Piu answered excitedly on his behalf.

"It's over eleven! When are we going to have our dinner?" My hunger coupled with the fear that something may go wrong spoke.

"Don't worry bhabhi, we shall have a short drinks session. Moreover, there are so many items; it will get wasted," Anurag said.

"The night is still young, Amy. Let's just enjoy!" Piu joined him immediately to persuade me.

"I don't like this," I whispered in Shashank's ear.

"It's alright, honey. We will just take a couple of drinks and get it done with." He held my hand and gave a tap of assurance.

I agreed half-heartedly.

"Can we start?" Piu seemed hyperenthusiastic. It was her first night out in our hometown and maybe, she wanted it to be the best.

She handed me the glass the moment I forced my thumbs up. Anurag took out kebabs and chillies and served.

"Cheers!" Piu's voice surpassed all as we raised the toast for the second time that evening.

Things had been pretty decent until my third peg, as far as I could recall. We talked about our college, classmates, professors, Anurag's business and so on.

"I think that's enough!" I said in a slurry voice. I was feeling extremely light, as if I was floating in the air. I had already started losing control of my limbs. The glass fell on the floor as I tried to keep it on the table after my third drink.

"Just one more, bhabhi!" Anurag said as he opened the bottle.

"Let it be, Anu! She has had enough," Shashank stopped him.

I think that the boys had already gulped down six pegs until then.

"A small one, from my side. Please, for our friendship!" Anurag wasn't ready to take no for an answer.

"Okay okay, but wonly a liiitlee," I said.

"But," I continued, "I need to pee first." I tried to get up; stumbled and failed miserably in my attempt of getting my heavy ass up.

"I got you!" My man caught me from out of nowhere.

"Owww, my baby. Thank you. I love you sooooo much," I said and gave him a peck.

He smiled and helped me to the washroom. I remember him watching over me like a guardian angel as I emptied my bladder.

We got back and guzzled the *official* last peg. My memory started to black out after that and all I could recollect were the bits and pieces of information. What I did recall vividly was – that wasn't our last drink!

I remember dancing with Shashank on some random songs and kissing him multiple times, while he got down on his knees more than once, declaring that I was the best thing that had ever happened to him. Even Anurag and Piu paired up for a couple of dances.

We played 'truth and dare' but I had no memory of what truth I revealed or the dare that I completed, or what any of them said or did. The mess in the place suggested that some pigs had eaten there last night. I was definitely the part of the herd but didn't know if I had my dinner with them. I remember checking my phone exactly at 1:30 a.m. When and how I reached the bedroom, or who got me there (it must have been Shashank) still escaped me.

My head was killing me and so was my body. It felt like I had been hit by a truck or something last night.

'God! I will never drink like this ever again.' I promised myself, feeling shittier than before and walked towards the kitchen to make some lemonade. My tummy was overfilled with water, yet I felt excessively thirsty.

I took out the last piece of lemon from the refrigerator, squeezed it in cold water. The mess in the living room made me feel sicker, so I went back to the bedroom and sat down on the bed, leaning comfortably against the head board while sipping the refreshing drink.

I applied a pain balm on my forehead and felt better after peeing a couple of times.

"Where is Piu?" It suddenly struck me as I got a grip of things.

My thought process was interrupted by some faint noise outside. I got up immediately and went to the door expecting Shashank to have come back from his workout, just to find Anurag.

"Hey! Good morning. Where did you go so early?" I asked.

"Good morning! Just went out to get some fresh air. My mind and body felt fucked up."

"Yeah! Even I need some," I said rubbing my forehead, trying to get some relief.

"Get some water! It will help," He said.

"The amount of water I have put in my body this morning has surpassed the total amount of water I have drank in the last ten days," I jeered.

He laughed and said, "Get some rest then. You will be fine."

"Yes, I will. Anyway, where is Shashank?" I asked.

"No idea! I should be asking you this." He sounded surprised.

"I don't know. He was not in bed when I got up. I thought he must have gone out for his workout," I said, a feeling concerned.

"He was pretty wasted last night. There is no way he can work out," he said.

"Are you absolutely sure he didn't wake up before you, Anurag?" I asked agitatedly.

"Of course, I unlocked the door and the gate," he replied

"Where is he?" I started getting anxious.

"Don't worry, Amyra! He must be lying somewhere around in the house," Anurag continued, "I will check the guest room."

"Did you not sleep there?" I asked him.

"Nope! I found myself on this sofa this morning," he said, scratching his head and looking away to hide the embarrassment.

"How did you sleep on all this, Anurag?" It seemed preposterous but who was I to judge! I was no better last night.

"I was fully tanked Amyra!" he answered, irritated.

"Okay, sorry. Don't get mad!" I apologised.

"It's okay! Now let's look for the lost soul."

"Okay, and where is Piu?" I asked him.

"She may be in Shashank's mom's room. That is where he planned to let your friends sleep," he said.

"Okay! I will check the guest room," I said, walking towards it, while Anurag went to the kitchen saying, "I will get some water."

The door of the guest room was shut, but not locked from inside. I went in slowly to wake him up, just to find the room too neat to have been used by anyone last night. The washroom door was wide open and I peeped in to be sure. He wasn't there. There was only one more room left to check.

Suddenly, an unpleasant thought got into my mind and made me panic. I ran frantically towards Shashank's mom's room.

"Lord, I wanna be wrong. Please god," I murmured while wiping the sweat on my forehead along the way.

"Hey Amyra! Wait, what's wrong?" Anurag shouted and followed as he saw me scuttling through like crazy. I reached the door and pushed it wide open.

19

Life Wrecked

The sight inside the room turned my life upside down completely. I froze and my legs gave up. Anurag caught me from behind as I lost my balance.

Piu and Shashank were sleeping together hugging each other, just like us. The structure of their intertwined bodies were perceptible even from the blanket that covered them neck below.

I walked forward slowly, trembling like a leaf, and gradually pulled the blanket to see the most heart-breaking vision of my life. My life wrecked like a ship that collided with an ice-berg at its top speed.

"Fuck man!" Anurag shouted right behind me as I howled, "This isn't true. It's a dream. It's just a stupid nightmare, right Anurag? Pinch me. Wake me up, please!"

I was devastated and had no control over my tears. He hugged me wordlessly. His shirt got wet with my tears.

Time had stopped; my heart had shattered into a million pieces. My lover and my best friend had backstabbed me. All my dreams faded into thin air.

"Please mom! Wake me up; somebody please wake me up!" I pleaded. I wasn't ready to accept that truth.

"Shashank! Wake up, you fucker!" Anurag shouted and hit him.

Things turned from bad to worse as his action further revealed their unresponsive bare bodies on one another.

"Fuck!" I screamed, covered my eyes and ran out of the room. I reached Shashank's bedroom and locked the door from inside.

"Amyra! Please open the door. Don't do anything stupid." Anurag banged the door and shouted.

"I am changing!" I tried to yell, but my voice was strangled in my throat. I washed my face, changed and got out of the room immediately.

Anurag stood outside the room.

"I will drop you home," he said anxiously.

"Thanks Anurag, but I can manage." I tried hard not to cry, but failed miserably.

"It's too early to find public transport," he insisted.

"Please, just let me go." I pleaded with folded hands, wiping the tears off my face.

"Okay!" he said and continued, "I am sorry that you had to go through this because of my friend."

"Please stop it yaa! I don't have anything to do with you or your friend or that bitch," I said while walking rapidy towards the door.

Suddenly, I stopped near the door and said, "On second thought, I want you to do something for me."

"Yes Amyra, anything you say," he said.

"When he gets up, just tell him that Amyra thanked him for everything and he can fuck that fucking bitch as much as he wants from now on. As a matter of fact, he can fuck any bitch he wants any number of times. I don't fucking care."

I sat down by the door and started crying outrageously for the next couple of minutes as he sat beside me like a mannequin.

"Can you do it for me?" I asked.

"Yes!" he replied apologetically.

"Thanks," I said.

"Amyra, I think you should talk to him once," Anurag said while I walked towards the gate.

"Do you think there's still anything left to talk? You are making me sick. Just fuck off!" I shouted at him and darted out.

I walked down the road crying bitterly. There was nothing that could help me stop those tears flooding out of my eyes. Passers-by looked at me and talked among themselves. I didn't care; my shame was overwhelmed by my intense agony.

I stood by the pavement and booked a cab online that was three minutes from my location. My phone rang.

"Hello ma'am, it's the driver. Where are you?" A light voice on the other side asked.

"I am right here on the main road." I looked around to find a few cars speeding around.

"Are you dressed in a red kurti and white cardigan, ma'am?"

"Yes!"

Within moments, a white car came and stopped by me. I checked the number plate and entered it.

"Where to, ma'am?" The middle-aged driver asked me gently.

"Anandpur chowk. I'll tell you the way after that," I replied.

"Okay!" He said and started driving.

I looked out of the window, staring at the happy faces, stray dogs, newspaper hawkers, closed shops, open milk parlours, the pathway, the trees, the birds and other vehicles that passed by speedily. Tears kept rolling down my cheeks all over again.

Everyone was happy, except me.

Suddenly my phone rang; it was mom. I did not want to take the call, but that would make her worried, so I picked it up and tried to sound as normal as possible. "Hello mom. Good morning!"

"Hello, good morning beta! Where are you?" she asked.

"At Varsha's place, mom." I did not know why I said that.

"Are you okay, Amy?" she asked.

I wanted to say, "No mom, I am not okay!" Instead, I said, "I am fine mom, why?"

"Just had a bad feeling. Anyway, come home soon! I have a surprise for you," she said.

A special telepathy operates among the people who love you. They can easily sense when you are in trouble, no matter how far you are from them.

"You are home?" I was surprised.

"Yes kiddo! Now come to your mama. It seems I haven't seen you for months. Missing you!" she said lovingly.

I wanted to run and hug her at that moment.

"Me too, mom. I will be there soon," I said, trying hard to control the sudden outburst of my tears.

"What would you like to have for breakfast?"

"Anything..."

"Okay. See you, Amy."

"Bye mama!"

I was overwhelmed with emotions; cheated by my partner and backstabbed by my bestie. But I still had my mother's love.

However, my feeble mind was back to focussing on my pain for the rest of the drive. I was neither sleeping nor awake; neither feeling nor thinking. Maybe, I was lost in an unknown dimension.

I told the driver to drop me a few hundred meters away from my house. There was no way I wanted to get in front of my mom like that.

It was 7:15 a.m. when I stepped out of the cab. And the first thing I did was call Oli.

She picked it up almost immediately and said sleepily, "Hello bitch, are you pregnant already?"

Her voice made me burst into tears instantaneously.

"Hel…o…!" The cry stifled my voice and the words managed to leave arduously.

"Hello, Amy. Is everything alright?" She was alarmed.

"Aham. I…. broke up with him!" I cleared my throat and said it hastily.

"What? Why?" I couldn't speak at all. "Amy, where are you?" she continued asking questions in shock and disbelief as I continued crying.

"I am near Mamta Stationery," I said trying to control myself.

"Okay. Stay there! I will come in five minutes," she said.

"No, I will come to your place," I said and headed towards her house.

I was there in five minutes and found her waiting for me in her night dress with a cardigan and a shawl at the doorsteps. Tears exploded uncontrollably from my eyes again as I saw her.

I wiped my face and put on a fake smile because her mom was home.

"Hey! C'mon in." She started ushering me in.

"Where is aunty?"

"Don't worry about her. She is in the kitchen."

"Okay."

We entered and headed towards her room straightaway. Things had become too burdensome for me to endure by then and I broke down. I hugged her and started weeping bitterly. She hugged me tight and brushed my hair speechlessly as my endless tears fell on her cardigan.

After a long spell of ceaseless crying, she made me sit on her bed and gave me a glass of water. I drank some of it as she sat down on the floor in front of me with her palms on my thighs.

She wiped my tears and asked me, "You look like shit. What happened, Amy? Even though I was high, things seemed fine to me as far as I could recollect."

"Things were exceptionally good…" I started the story from the time Anurag and Piu came back after dropping her home and narrated the whole story to her in a single breath with consistent tears. Her eyes got wider with shock and disbelief by the end.

Pin drop silence filled the room for the next couple of minutes as she tried to digest the stuff that had just been forced into her.

"Oli, come here!" It was her mom. She wanted her in the kitchen.

"Coming, mom!" she replied.

"Sorry Amy, I will be back in a minute," she said and left the room.

I took out my phone and started checking my gallery that was filled with my pics with him. I scrolled down and relived the memories that had become a torture by then.

"Stop doing this to yourself, Amy!" Oli came and snatched the phone from my hand.

"I can't help it yaa. I love him so much!"

I started thumping the floor with my legs. "Why Oli, why did he do this to me? Why did Piu do this to me? She was our best friend. They backstabbed me ruthlessly. What did I do to them to deserve this?" I continued and started crying desolately in my agony.

"All will be good." Even she started crying in my anguish and hugged me tight.

"I wanna die yaa!" I wailed.

"Don't you dare think like that, Amy. Ever! Remember that your mother lives for you. Think about the struggles and hardships she underwent to raise you after your father passed away. Don't you dare undermine her love like that because of some bastards!"

I cried and nodded my head, understanding what she had just told me.

The room echoed with our sobs for the next few minutes.

"Mom is home. I don't want to face her like this!" I said while wiping the tears off my face. Oli's contention about mom gave me some courage and strength.

"Yeah! You look like shit. Mom will freak out if she sees you like this."

"Exactly!"

"I thought you told me yesterday that she was supposed to reach by evening?"

"Yes, but there might have been some change in the programme. She called me while I was on my way back," I told her.

"Okay, so you wanna freshen up now?" she asked.

"In a few minutes, Oli."

"Okay! This is your home and..."

I interrupted her, "I know that I can stay here for as long as I want to. You don't need to say that, Oli."

"Yes! That's like my Amy." She smiled at me.

"Even Shashank told me that his house was mine..." I started crying again.

"Hey babe, he does not deserve this much attention." She hugged me.

"The fact that it was Piu, our best friend, is killing me. This is so fucking painful, Oli." I started yelping like an injured puppy.

She continued rubbing my back and scalp wordlessly.

"Fuck them, Amy!" There was a lot of rage in her voice.

"Yes, fuck those bastards! They don't deserve my tears," I said trying to cope up. "Let's talk about something else, Oli."

"Okay," she said trying to figure out something to say.

"I hope nobody came to know that you got drunk yesterday," I started.

"Nope, I was completely in my senses by the time I reached home."

"Okay, I was a bit worried. You seemed very high."

"Yup, but everything turned out to be good in the end."

"Yeah, everything turned out to be good for everyone, except me."

I was again sliding back when Oli interrupted, "Amy!"

"I am sorry. I am unable to help it. Sorry to bother you so much." My helpless voice was a mixture of apology, regret and pain.

"You need not be sorry for anything. I can understand," she said with all the love and affection she could have put in those words.

"Thanks, Oli!"

"From when did we start using words like 'thanks' and 'sorry', yaa?"

"Okay… sorry!"

"Again!"

"Okay!" I held my hands up with a weak smile. "I should get freshened up!" I said.

"Hmm. I will take care of a few morning chores by then," she said and stood up.

"No problem!" I said, combing my bag for my toothbrush as she left the room and I proceeded to the washroom.

I looked at myself in the mirror and was filled with disgust for defiling myself at his hands.

'You should die, Amyra!' It was a loud voice playing in my head.

I was shaken, "What wrong did I do to deserve that?"

'This is the end of the line for you, Amyra! Shashank cheated on you because you weren't good enough and you never will be good enough for anyone in the world. You are not going to be loved by anyone, ever. You are a fucking loser!'

I covered my ears and said out loud, "Stop it!"

But the voices continued, 'You should die.'

'Maybe a boy may never love me; I may not be good enough to please others, but I know that my mother loves me like no other and she wouldn't ever cheat on me. This is reason enough for me to live, love her and give her all the happiness that she had devoid herself from to keep me happy.' I refuted strongly and the voices faded away.

The words rejuvenated me and I finally decided to focus on getting ready for mom.

How delusional was my thought of my love story being the perfect one. I felt like the most special lady to have taken birth on this planet. We created new memories every day. Everyone was envious of my love story. However, everything was devastated in a moment. I knew then that mine was the most 'imperfect love story'.

20

I am sorry, Mom!

14 January 2018

9:00 a.m.

My usually cheerful neighbourhood was still and gloomy. The silence was inexplicable. None of the children played around; birds did not sing; people walked around mutely; stray dogs coiled and sat silently near the walls trying to get some sun.

The pleasant aroma of *chhole* filled my nostrils as I reached the door sluggishly and knocked.

"Who is it?" Mom shouted from inside.

"It's me," I replied.

She opened the door in a minute and I walked in, trying to avoid eye contact with her.

"What happened, Amy?" she asked the moment she saw me.

"Nothing mom. Why?" I said looking away from her.

"You have cried a lot. Your eyes are swollen," she said anxiously.

Her words broke me down and I started weeping immediately.

"What's wrong?" She looked into my eyes affectionately and asked.

"I am sorry, mom! I made a terrible mistake." The words came out involuntarily as I wiped my tears and continued, "I lied to you about last night. We were not at Varsha's house."

"Then?"

I meant no disrespect, but I did not have the guts to look at her face. "We were at Shashank's place," I said with a loud sigh among my cry.

"Who is Shashank?" she asked.

"He is a professor in our college. I had been dating him since last year."

"Professor!" She exclaimed with her eyes wide open.

"Yes mom."

"You *had* been dating… means you broke up with him?" she asked, trying to figure out the things.

"Yes, this morning," I replied with tear-filled eyes.

"May I ask why?" she enquired.

"Mom, can we please save that for later?" I pleaded.

"Okay, but there is something I need you to tell me now."

I had a fairly good idea of what she might ask and was ready with an answer; another white lie.

"You were with him the whole night. Did you guys—?" She was straightforward.

"No mom!" I told her right away. There was no way I could have told her how intimate we were.

"Thank god!" She sighed.

"But…" A single word created great many fringes of worries across her face as she looked at me.

"We kissed and had alcohol. I am so sorry, mom." I got down on my knees with folded hands.

My eyes were fixed at her feet as she said, "So this is the reason you look like shit! But I wanna know what happened that led to your sudden breakup?" Mom said grimly.

I knew that there was no way I could have procrastinated. I sat down on the floor and articulated the whole incident to her disconsolately.

"How dare he do this to my daughter?" She was vexed and continued in her rage, "And I never expected this from Piu." My mom had her eyes filled with tears of concern, pain and anger. "A couple of backstabbers! You are not going to be associated with those pricks."

"I won't," I said weepily.

She hugged me and continued, "And I am going to ensure that."

I did not completely understand what she meant by that.

"I am sorry, mom. So sorry." I had kept my eyes shut, but the tears found their way. She picked me up gently by my shoulders, looked into my eyes and said with a smile, "It's okay baby!"

Was it really okay? I had not expected her to be that understanding at all. Maybe, that's where we misjudge our parents. "Are you not mad at me, mom?" I asked apprehensively.

"Well, I am not particularly proud of what you have done; but I appreciate you telling me the truth."

Her words stung me because I had not been completely honest with her, but I had no other option. I did not have the guts.

"Well! I am starving. Can we eat?" she said, trying to change the topic.

I tagged along. "Yes! What's along with chhole?"

"So, you already know about it?"

"Yup!"

"I have kneaded the dough for your favourite *puri*."

"Wow! You are the best, mom," I said and hugged her.

She hugged me back and said affectionately, "My baby, now go and get changed. I will get the puris ready in the meantime."

"Okay mom!" I said and walked towards my bedroom.

It took me less than two minutes to get myself into comfortable clothes and I threw myself into my bed lifelessly.

"Amy, get up! Breakfast is ready." The voice startled me and it took me a minute to realise that I had dozed off.

1:30 p.m.

Mom, Oli and I sat together in a circle on the floor, surrounding the food items for our lunch. Mom had prepared paneer curry, pulses, salad and papad, while Oli made a special sweet sauce she had learnt from YouTube.

I felt a lot better after getting some sleep and a relaxing shower. Oli had come home when I was in my deep sleep mode. We were just about to have our lunch when someone banged our door, "Amy… Amy…!"

That was him and I turned pale.

"So, it's Shashank, right?" Mom asked looking into my eyes.

"Yes," I replied anxiously. That was the last thing expected out of him.

"Why is he here now? I will go and slap him right now." Oli got up, prepared to go out.

"No! I will take care of him. I suggest the two of you go into the bedroom," Mom said sternly.

We followed her instruction instantly as she went to get the door.

I took out my headphone, plugged it into my ears and started listening to some music at a high volume immediately. There was no way I wanted to hear anything that was going on outside.

'Why did he have to come here? Can't he let me live in peace?' The thoughts agonized me even in midst of heavy music that filled in my ears.

I took out my headphones when mom entered the room after long twenty to twenty-five minutes. She said, "I made him leave." There was again a pin drop silence.

"What did he say?" I asked.

"He said nothing, just insisted on talking to you, and said that he loved you!"

"Love, my foot! There is nothing left to talk with him after what I saw…" My voice got choked again.

She was infuriated and said, "How can a person be this shameless? He should have never showed his face to you after performing such an ugly act."

"Our food must have turned cold. I will heat it up," Oli said and walked to the kitchen to give the mother-daughter duo some privacy.

Mom continued as Oli went out, "I know this isn't going to be easy for you, Amy, but you have to do this. Your eyes tell me that you were deeply involved with him, but it's time to let it go as what happened can never be repaired."

She added further, "And this, honey, is not the time to lose yourself. It's a time for a radical shift in persective. I have tried to give you the best and I know it's not enough. But you are much better than me. You can have a life I could only dream of providing you. You have a long life ahead of you and I want to see you in that position before I take my last breath. You have a chance to focus on more important things of life which you might have missed – your studies and career."

"You have given me everything and even more, mom. You are the best!"

I held her hand as she said, "Okay! So now, be a strong girl and show the two-timers that you are unstoppable."

"Yes, mama." I wiped my face.

"I think we should join Oli, or else she would starve to death waiting for the mother-daughter talk to get over."

21

Life without Him

My life underwent a significant change after the breakup. The usual fidgety me was transformed into an aimless sloth who wasted hours after hours, just by staring at the walls. Oli tried to cheer me up by taking me to cool places while mom prepared my favourite dishes all the time.

Despite their efforts, things did not seem to work well for me, mostly because of the loss of desire to move on. I had got into the toxic habit of self-pitying and hated hanging out, for it brought back Shashank's memories. There was not a single place left in Ranchi where I had not been with him.

My loving gesture to feed Shashank with the first bite whenever we ate together, haunted me every time I ate. I had turned into a lonely soul as tears flowed uninhibitedly. So much so, that my pillow was consistently damp and had started to fade.

Mornings and nights – the time we used to talk and video chat – were the most difficult. I dearly missed him and was unable to help thinking what he might be doing then. His daily routine was on my fingertips. He often told me that his food didn't go down well until he heard my voice. Sometimes, I even wondered how his stomach might be working without me. So stupid of me to have fallen for his charms!

Whenever I got hiccups, the thought of 'he is missing me really bad' occupied my mind.

I did all the things to get rid of his memories. I deleted all our pics, blocked him on Facebook, Instagram and WhatsApp accounts, changed my number and deleted my email ID. However, there are no shift+delete buttons for human minds as it has the tendency to linger on past memories, causing the heart to break with unrequited longing.

Strangely, we had no whereabouts of Piu. It was nothing like I wanted her to come and apologize to me, but somewhere deep inside, we expected her to show up. Either she was too ashamed to face us, or she did not care at all.

14 February 2018

2:00 p.m.

It had been exactly one month since our breakup, but my mind and soul were still trapped in the memories of 14 January 2018. Minutes passed like hours, hours felt like days and days seemed like months. A typical day in my life had me getting up in the morning, eating, staring at the books, crying recurrently and sleeping.

Oli was my faithful accomplice throughout. In fact, the only reason of my little academic progress in those days was attributed to her presence and encouragement.

On the day of submission of projects, she went to the college all by herself, because I had no intention of going anywhere near our college. Anyway, that did not help much, as my mind moved around college and him. Oli saw Piu in college and said, "The bitch had no remorse on her face. She saw right through me and was having a merry time with Maddy."

I couldn't help but ask her about Shashank, to which she replied that he had been on an indefinite leave. 2 February 2018, fifteen minutes past three in the afternoon, marked our very last conversation about them.

And there I was, standing meekly after thirty days of anguish, melancholy and loneliness; ready for the next level of the game – Valentine's Day.

The day when millions of love birds around the universe were chirping, frolicking and flying around gleefully, I sat in the company of my agony, shedding tears over the memories of the previous year.

22

Valentine's Week, 2017

I was having the time of my life with Shashank. There wasn't a single day we did not meet after the classes. Sona Towers, a shopping complex near Lalpur, had become our meeting point. Saturday was rechristened by us as our 'Date-day'. We used to go out on lunch dates, movie dates, coffee dates, drink dates and sometimes combining one with the other, painting the town red with our love. Unlike others, I used to wait excitedly for Mondays as we were usually unable to meet on Sundays.

We were wired 24x7. Nights used to be filled with schmoozes until we dozed off with headphones, still plugged into our ears. I had immersed myself into the ocean of my newly-found love, discovering exciting things every moment. Every word spoken by the man, every bit of his action made me feel like a queen. Nobody had made me feel that special ever and I relished every moment, falling more in love.

Valentine's week had been particularly special.

On rose day, I got a beautiful pink rose after the class. This was apart from virtual roses that decorated my phone early in the morning and throughout the day.

The next day was propose day, and he behaved pretty strange that day. His texts were limited to one word answers – 'Yes', 'No' and 'Okay'. His attitude towards me, in college, was a bit puzzling. I felt as if he was trying to avoid me all the time. There were no usual winks and kisses. It was towards the end of the class that I received his text, *See you in Sona at four.*

So, there I was in front of Sona. My phone vibrated as I looked around. It was Shashank.

"Hello!" I said.

"Hey!"

"Where are you?" I asked looking around, trying to locate him.

"Right behind you." I turned around to find him waving his hand at me from his car and walked towards him.

"Come in!" He opened the door for me and said frigidly. That was not how he usually was. Something was definitely not right and I asked him affectionately, "You can tell me if there's a problem, babe."

"Hmm" He buzzed softly with his gaze fixed on the road.

I thought it better to remain silent and shifted my focus to the road.

"Where are we going?" Words came out helplessly from my lips.

"You will know soon," he replied briefly with mystifying words.

I was wondering what was going on in his mind, as he applied brakes in the parking lot of Anand Park. I was very surprised because parks were the last places he wanted to visit. We walked silently along the tiled pathway and took a seat on one of the benches in a grassy area.

"Are you alright?" I asked and he pointed towards the right side in reply.

I turned my head and squealed in excitement.

There was a golden Labrador pup with a placard in its neck that said,

Amyra,
I love you
Will you be mine?

"Yes, yes, yes. I am only yours." I turned with moistened eyes and found him on his knees with a paper in his hands. He started reading before I could have said anything,

I want the terrene encapsulated within your eyes,
To be my world forever,
The lax darkness of your locks overwhelming me,
As I close my eyes in savour.
I want to see your eyes as sunrise every morning,
And as sunset in the evening,
Dive into the deep recesses of your heart and bring out,
Priceless hidden treasures within.
I want to be drenched with the streams of love,
Flowing through your lips,
The cleft in my palms be filled with your fingers
As we say "I do", witnessed by our kins!

That was immensely endearing and there was no way I could have stopped myself from getting down on my knees and hugging him.

"I love you! I love you so much babe. Thanks a lot." I did not know what to say. Those words came out of my lips spontaneously.

On Chocolate day, he sent a set of five Cadbury Dairy Milk Silk chocolates for me and two, each for Oli and Piu. On Teddy day, a key chain with an adorable white teddy holding a velvet red heart that said, "I love you" came my way. And, it became an inseparable part of my college bag forever since that day.

11 February was Promise day, and he handed me a thoughtful card sketched by him that portrayed a boy and a girl holding hands and walking merrily on a road towards a beautiful sunrise. It had a quote that said, 'I promise to keep you safe and happy while walking by your side until my last breath.'

On Hug day, I got a text early in the morning that day. *Hey babe, meet me at the Firayalal Chowk at ten today.*

What's the plan? I asked.

I'll tell you when we meet.

Typical mysterious Shashank! Sometimes I hated the suspense that he created every now and then, but I loved the surprises.

I replied, *Okay!*

Please put on an Indian attire.

Why? Are you taking me to meet your mom? I pinged with a wink.

Not today. His text had a smile emoji.

And there I was, three hours after that conversation, in his car, heading towards an unknown destination.

He did not even drop a hint as to where we were headed, and finally, he slowed down after thirty minutes. I stepped out to find a five feet by three feet white tin board that said, 'Mohit's Orphanage' in blue paint.

I felt at sea and asked, "Why are we here?"

"Have some patience, sweetheart!"

I rolled my eyes at him, which he did not see.

We walked through a small space that seemed overly congested by a couple of seesaws and a metallic slide, that were put together in between an L-shaped asbestos, building within the campus.

"Hello Amyra didi!" A mixed voice of over twenty-five children, aged between five to ten years, who had accommodated themselves skilfully in a way that left a big space in the front echoed in my ears as soon as I entered through a dirty green wooden door.

I was stunned to hear my name and looked at Shashank. He smiled and took me by hand towards a small table that had some food packets and a cake placed on it.

"Hello everyone!" I replied nervously, trying to compose myself.

I was still trying to get my heads around the things that were going on when an old woman, clad in white sari, who stood by the side of the table came near and opened the packet that contained a delicious looking heart-shaped vanilla cake that said, "Happy Hug Day Amyra".

I was speechless at the amazingly charming display of love. The lady handed a fibre knife and asked me to cut the cake.

"Join me, baby!" I said.

Shashank held my hand as we cut the cake. A loud round of applause continued as we gave a small bite to each other.

"Distribute the packets, Amy!" he whispered in my ears.

"Okay!" I felt super-special as the children lined themselves up to receive those from me.

First in the line was a girl who gave me a hug before receiving the packet. The process continued and I had already received genuine hugs of gratitude and love from over twenty-five children. My eyes dampened with a plethora of feelings comprising of joy, pride, gratitude, inspiration and above all, love.

A tight hug outside the campus by my love with a whisper, "Happy hug day, sweetheart!" garnished the awesomeness of that day. I cannot think of a hug day that could have been more special than that.

A long smooch that lasted over thirty minutes (it's no exaggeration) behind a big rock in "Rock Garden" marked the celebration of my first Kiss Day.

The big day had finally arrived. My first ever Valentine's day as a couple!

We had planned to meet after my classes (as usual) that I was in no mood to attend. However, he did not have the flexibility to bunk the classes, so I had to wait until 3:30 p.m.

I packed my favourite black dress in the college bag to get changed after my classes in Rishika's room. She was the most reticent girl in the class who acquainted everyone, but befriended none. I was lucky to get permission to use her room after the classes a day before.

I was on my way to Lalpur in an auto-rickshaw, running behind time. Rishika had been kind enough to let me use few of her cosmetics, apart from her room and washroom. It had been a pleasant experience, knowing her that day. She also obliged me by getting a pretty red rose from the garden at the backyard of her hostel.

I looked at my phone anxiously as it was 3:15 p.m. already. Just then, the driver entered a petrol pump. Damn! I wanted to punch that fellow. These things are always bound to happen when you are running late.

Finally, I was there with him, tearing through all the obstacles and relaxing in the comfortable ambience of the car.

"Relax, you look exhausted," he said and handed a bottle of water to me.

"Really?" I said and pulled down the vanity mirror in the car reflexively to check on myself, taking the bottle in one hand. The heat and dust, coupled with my anxiety, had got me looking weary and oily. I took out tissue papers and cleaned my face immediately as he fired the ignition.

I sipped the water and asked, "So, what's the plan today baby?"

He replied with a wink, "Sit back and enjoy the drive, babe. You will know soon!"

There was no point in asking him any further. So, I engaged myself with some cosmetic touch-up to ensure his undivided attention as we cruised down the road.

"Your attention should be on the road, Mr Shashank Raj." I teased him as he was caught red-handed, checking me out from the corner of his eyes.

"Do you have a problem with that Ms Amyra?"

"No, not at all." I blushed and thought, 'That's what I want!'

"So, you can permit me to continue checking you out and drink in your beauty," he whispered leaning close.

His unorthodox sexiness was turning me on.

I kissed his ear and said, "I love you!"

"I love you too!"

Close to forty-five minutes later, we went off-road through some village and farmlands to reach a riverside. Shashank applied brakes and brought the car to a standstill, after taking a U-turn by the bank.

"Wow! What place is this?" I asked, admiring the beauty of the place.

"I am not very sure of the name, but this area is called Sukurhuttu," he told me.

"Okay, can you please unlock the door? I want to feel the freshness outside." I was tempted to get my feet in the water.

"I am afraid, you'll have to wait inside for a couple of minutes, baby."

"Why?" I asked quizzically.

"I have a surprise for you," he said in his typical mischievous style.

"I thought this was the surprise!"

"I will be back in a jiffy," he continued. "And please don't look back."

"Okay Mr Shashank, I won't." I closed my eyes and reclined comfortably on the seat.

The sound and movement of him opening the trunk and taking out stuff prompted me to get a bit nosy, but the incredibly honest Amyra prevailed, 'He is doing it for you and you have no right to spoil the surprise.'

However, I sneak peaked through the rear view mirror, just to get a glimpse of his brow.

I looked at the beauty around, not looking behind. I realised it was just a rivulet; most probably a tributary of some bigger river.

The area on our side of the brook was mostly farmland while, that on the other side looked akin to a mini jungle. Light fog drifted across the water, reducing the visibility across.

A serene island crammed with bushes and rocks had come up right at the centre. I started day-dreaming about being stranded in it for life. It would be our small world, with no outside interference. Just the two of us – eating, sleeping, making love, raising our kids and enjoying every moment with each other.

"Step out of the car, babe!"

Finally, Shashank released me from captivity and I breathed in fresh air which was not so common in the city.

He blindfolded me with his fingers, the moment I stepped out the and made me walk approximately fifty steps. My hair fluttered and dress billowed around me from the cold breeze.

"Ready, babe? One, two, three!" he said and removed his hands from my eyes.

I was elated to be the guest of honour to a largely photogenic arrangement that revealed itself.

"Oh my god!" I was completely awestruck.

"Happy Valentine's day!" he said and gave me a red rose with droplets of water sparkling all around it.

"Happy Valentine's day to you too!" I kissed the rose and replied.

A miniature circular wooden table was placed on a rectangular sea green mat big enough to accommodate the two of us. A dark green-coloured bottle of champagne was placed at the centre with two glasses on either side that reflected the orange rays of the sun exquisitely. The entire setup was made amidst two hand, pedalled blue and red boats, the beaks of which converged at a sixty degree angle.

An "S" was embossed on the sandy space between the table setup and the beaks. Suddenly, I noticed that the boats formed an

"A" and housed the "S". I was speechless at the enchanting movie style arrangement made by him.

"Thank you, sweetheart. You are my angel," my voice choked.

"You are welcome, baby."

"Before you say anything else or come up with any more surprises," I interrupted him, got down on my knees and presented the rose saying, "I love you with all my heart, soul and body, Mr Shashank Raj. I don't have anything else to offer, but this petite flower and me."

He got down on his knees and took the drop of tear running out of my eyes on his fingers and said, "Whoa! Don't lose these pearls now. You shall need a lot of them during your farewell when I steal you from your mom."

I smiled softly at his captivating words. He said lovingly, in his voice as soft as dew, "This petite flower is the most precious gift and you are all I need to live."

He came closer to me and his fragrance filled my nostrils. I closed my eyes as his lips brushed against mine.

"Are you always going to love me this much?" I asked.

"No, that's not possible," he said.

The answer was quite unexpected and I breathed out dejected as he continued, "I love you more with every passing moment. So technically, I cannot love you the same. It's going to escalate and I can't help it!"

A hundred cupids had hit my heart with their arrows by the time he finished his sentence.

I was intoxicated. "Please don't change, I won't survive without you!"

"I won't," he replied.

"Thank you for everything, babe!" I said and hugged him tighter.

"You are welcome, my love." A cute smile accompanied his reply.

23

His pen... our Love Story!

1 January 2019/ Present day

10:07 a.m.

"Who's there?" Oli shouted as I knocked at the door.

"It's me," I replied.

The door opened in the next few seconds and an excessively excited Oli emerged with a hoot and hugged me tight. "Haaaappy Neeeew Yeeeear, Amy."

I hugged her back and screamed, "Haaaappy Neeeeew Yeeeeear."

All the heads turned towards us as we shouted and snuggled in the veranda.

"Come in, bitch!" She chuckled.

It had been a long time since I had experienced the sheer joy of being slanged. My past experience had turned me into a touch-me-not and I retracted into my personal space. My conversations were heavily confined to academics. I was too afraid to make an affable move.

Oli's mom came out dressed up for work by the time I stepped into the sitting room.

"Happy New Year, aunty," I said and touched her feet.

"Happy New Year, Amy. God bless you. May you get all the happiness and success." She showered her blessings and hugged me.

"Thank you, aunty!"

"God! What have you done to yourself?"

I was surprised by her tone and started looking at myself, "What aunty?"

"Don't you get anything to eat in Bangalore? You look famished," she smirked.

"I eat a lot aunty, and as a matter of fact, I have gained a few kilos," I said defensively.

"Where?" She giggled mischievously and made me blush.

She said, "Amy, if you continue like this, you are going to be invisible someday."

"Mom! Forgive her," Oli came to my rescue.

"Where are you going, aunty?" I changed the topic.

"Work!" She said in a helpless tone.

"No leave?"

"Nope! I need to rush. You guys enjoy the day and don't forget to have *gulab jamuns.* They are in the refrigerator."

She said and left while we went to Oli's bedroom. The irresistibly cosy bed glazed with a baby pink mink blanket invited us to nuzzle.

I got rid of my cardigan immediately and curled into its warmth, "Wow!"

"Comfy?" She sneered.

"Absolutely! Now what were you were telling me about yesterday night?" I said, lolling further into the depths.

"Have patience! I should probably get you some sweets first," she said.

"Yeah, sure."

"And don't rub your filthy feet on my new bedsheet," she said playfully.

I showed her my middle finger in reply, to which she made faces.

"So what was it about?" I asked again, while striving to make sure that the syrup didn't spill over as I ate the fifth large-sized gulab jamun prepared by her mom.

The first day of the New Year had started with me cramming huge chunks of calories into my body. Chhole bhature was paired with rice pudding in my home and gulab jamuns paired with chocolate sponge cakes in hers.

She got up and took out a book from her bag and tossed it in front of me on the bed.

"All this suspense over a book!" I sneered.

But, things changed instantaneously as I picked it up.

The blue and white cover page had a dark shady image of a couple. They were stepping away from each other tearfully, but had their pinky fingers entwined. The top of the page contained the title of the book in black, *Love, Loss and Pain*, while the lower part had the name of the author, Shashank Raj.

Tears rolled down my eyes, all of a sudden. An inescapable landslide of intense pain and angst crushed me from all directions. The struggles to get over my agony turned futile in a second.

"Fuck yaa! Why did you have to show this to me?" I said and hurled the book out of the bedroom door.

Oli got up and brought the book back and said, "I think you should read it once."

"I do not wish to be associated with that motherfucker," I said, wiping my tears.

"I know, neither do I. But still, you should read it," she said calmly and placed it in front of me.

"Give me one good reason, Oli," I said, clearing my throat.

"Coz I feel that he has written your love story, but things seem different at the end," she said.

"I don't fucking care if it's our story. Moreover, I don't want to revisit those moments and punish myself again. It's so fucking painful, Oli." I said and tears welled out uncontrollably.

"I can understand, Amy. It's just that he has penned down the incidents chronologically and everything seemed quite relatable, except for that night," she said.

"I don't want to know what he has written. I saw the two cheaters sleeping together with my own fucking eyes. I don't think there is anything else for me to know." I started weeping outrageously as that miserable image danced mockingly in front of my eyes.

"Sorry Amy, I still feel you should read this once," she said.

"I want to go home," I said, trying to recompose myself.

"Okay, but wash your face first," she replied.

She placed the book in my hand when I came back from the washroom. "I am your friend Amy, and I love you. I really want you to read it."

"I know, Oli. But I don't know if I can do that," I said.

"No probs, honey. Keep the book with you for now. If you want, you can read it; if not, return it to me before leaving," she said calmly.

I bade her goodbye and took quick steps towards home.

The book was tossed to the farthest corner of my table, the moment I stepped into my room. Almost immediately, I threw myself into my bed, covered my face with a pillow and started crying vehemently. I was overpowered by the excruciating pain inside me. I started hitting the wooden frame of the bed with my fist, in my efforts to nullify it, by inflicting external pain on myself. But, all my efforts to heal myself were futile.

It was more than an hour of racking torment. "Enough is enough, Amy!" I said to myself and looked straight at the book that seemed to call me out loud. Without much thought, I got up, picked the book and started reading it back in the bed. I needed to know what that fucker had written about us.

The page about the author said, "An alumni of St. Stephen's College, Delhi and a full time faculty of St. Louis' College, Ranchi comes up with his first novel… blah blah blah.

I started flipping through the pages rapidly and a multitude of intense emotions surfaced as I sauntered through the chapters. I drowned deep into the past while reading our love story from his perspective. An unexpected smile appeared on my face as deeply buried fond memories floated up. A vivid and sensual description of the love-making part made me blush and feel embarrassed initially which was followed by anger. 'How dare he describe our sex scenes without my permission?'

However, I decided to let it go and moved further. Somehow, my love for him rekindled, until I reached the final chapters.

"What the fuck is this?" I said to myself while reaching the end of the book. It was close to midnight by then. I was exasperated and couldn't resist calling Oli. She picked up after a few rings and whispered, "Hello."

I said uneasily, "Hello, Oli."

"So, you read the whole book?" she asked.

"Yes, you were right. It is our story, except for the fictional and imaginary part at the end. I am pissed. How dare he write such stuff about me?" I said angrily.

"Yeah, I know. That's the reason I wanted you to read it," she added.

"Is he here in Ranchi?" I enquired.

"Maybe, but I am not sure. The college is closed for the winter break," she said.

"I want to meet and slap him."

"Are you sure?" she asked surprised.

"Of course, if the bastard wrote our story, it should have been authentic. He had no right to put all the blame on me. I will be relieved only after giving him a tight slap or two," I said, annoyed.

"Okay, we will figure it out tomorrow. Get some sleep now, Amy!" she said.

"I will go to his house tomorrow. Will you come with me?" I asked.

"Okay," she replied after a lapse of a few seconds.

"Come to my place by ten," I said.

"Okay sweetheart. Now get some sleep! Good night," she said dotingly.

"Okay, good night," I said and disconnected the call.

2 January 2019

10:00 a.m.

We were on our way to Shashank's house. Oli had come to my place at around 9:45 a.m.

Last night had been one of the longest nights of my entire life. I checked the time regularly and remembered seeing my phone last at quarter to six in the morning, after which I dozed off to wake up to the alarm at seven thirty.

My sleep-deprived body felt lethargic. I tried my best to conceal the dark circles around my swollen eyes by applying some effective makeup. There was no way he should believe that I am still mourning for him. I wanted to see regret in his eyes for cheating on me and understand that I was the biggest loss of his life.

While in the auto, I noticed once again how everybody seemed to be in a rush. The cold winter wind, unaffected by the bright sun, whacked against my face. Oli tried to start conversation a couple of times, but I was lost in my own world of dejection. She plugged headphones in her ears and got busy with some music. It took us more than forty-five minutes to reach his house due to the heavy morning traffic.

Shanti Niwas, his house, looked the same, except for the worn out paint. The fear of the unknown gripped me as we walked through the garden that looked drab and desolate. My legs turned shaky as I pressed the doorbell.

The loud bell turned me pale. "Oli, this was a bad idea. I don't want to do it."

"It's okay, Amy. We are here and there is no turning back," she replied.

"No, no. This is a mistake. Let's go back, please." I was scared to death and my voice trembled.

I turned around, ready to run back, when the door opened and Oli held my hand. "Yes, whom do you want?" It was his mom and I was not ready to face her.

"Hello aunty! Is Shashank sir home?" Oli asked.

"Yes, and you are?" she asked politely.

"We are his students from St Louis' College. Just came around to wish him happy new year," Oli replied.

"That's strange! He does not entertain his students at home. What's your name?"

"I am Olive and—"

"Why is your friend so reluctant to show her face?" she interrupted Oli, caught my shoulders and forced me to turn around.

"You are Amyra, right?" she asked.

"Yes!" I said nervously gazing at the floor.

Bam! A tight slap scurried across my face before I could think or say anything.

That was absolutely unexpected. I was dazed; stars and planets started frolicking around me which was followed by an acute sensation of pain and heat on my cheeks. I burst into tears immediately.

"How dare you!" Oli shouted as I pulled her, "Let's get out of here, Oli!"

"I have been waiting to do that from months," she said furiously.

"She did nothing to deserve it. It was your son's fault," Oli lost her cool completely.

"Let's go, Oli. We should not have come here." I wailed and tried to pull her with all my might.

"She destroyed his life. She dumped him, broke his heart. My ever happy and cheerful son is now a melancholic loner and an alcoholic." She started weeping.

"She did nothing, you old woman. Your son cheated on her. He slept with someone else right in front of her eyes," Oli shouted at the top of her voice while jolting away from my grip.

Bam! It was Oli who got another tight one this time as his mom yelled, "Don't you dare raise a finger on my son!"

"Enough is enough! Just because you are old does not give you the right to slap us for nothing!" I howled in tears while hugging Oli from a side.

"Nothing? You have no idea what he has been through, dammit! I heard him weeping all night. He disrupted all his contacts from the outside world and locked himself in the room after you ditched him like the other girl. A fitness freak like him dropped his gym membership and submerged himself into the ocean of alcohol. I did not have the courage to leave him alone. The fear of losing my son has been eating me day and night. Frightful dreams of finding him hanging by the fan and slashing his wrists have been haunting me for months," she said weeping inconsolably.

"None of that is her fault. It was your son's own doing," Oli said loudly.

"I tried to offer him help from professionals, but he denied that outrightly. I have been seeing my son falling apart bit by bit because of you," She said intensely while pointing her shivering finger towards me, without listening to Oli.

"Just call him out, and you will know the truth!" Oli said aggressively as I cried bitterly.

His mom replied, "No! I don't want him—"

She was suddenly interrupted by a familiar voice. "What's the matter, mom? Why is there so much commotion?"

I was shocked to see Shashank as he walked towards us in a grey t-shirt and navy blue shorts. He was frail and dishevelled. His face was covered with a thick beard. His dark brown eyes appeared small and pale.

He stumbled and saved himself from falling by holding on to a table as he saw me. His mom ran towards him and said, "Are you okay, son?"

"Yes mom, I am fine."

He came right in front of me and said, "Hey Amy! How are you?"

I wasn't prepared for that moment. As a matter of fact, I wasn't prepared for any event that unfolded since I reached there. Tears gushed out of my eyes frantically and my voice choked as I replied, "I am okay. What about you?"

"I am perfectly fine." He did his best to control his tears, but failed.

"Hey Oli, how are you?" he asked her.

"I am good," she replied plainly, still rubbing her cheeks.

"Mom, did you slap them?" he asked shocked, looking at our faces.

"Yes, and I can do it again," she said coldly.

"Mom, please go inside!" He started crying.

His mom tried to say something, but was stopped by his words. "Mom, please!" He pleaded while looking into her eyes.

She went inside murmuring, probably cursing me from her heart and soul.

"I am so sorry on her behalf," he said with folded hands, trying to control his tears.

"It's okay. She did what any mother would do. It's not her fault; it's yours," I said.

His brows locked up, his expression suddenly changing from apologetic to being offended at my words.

"My fault? That's something new. But okay, please come in!" he said, trying to get back his composure.

"It's okay, we can talk here," I said.

"It isn't okay for me. We can sit and talk," he insisted.

Oli and I looked at each other and went in.

"Would you like to have some water?" he asked.

All the good and bad memories spiralled down my mind in an instant as we took our seats on the sofa.

"No, we are not here for the pleasantries," Oli said coldly.

"Okay, so what reminded you girls of me after all these months?" he asked, coming straight to the point.

I took out the book and threw it at his face and said, "What the fuck is this?"

"It's a book, written by me."

"It's not just a book. It's a story, our story," I shouted.

"So, you read the book!"

"Yes, and how dare you sell lies related to me? If you were a real man, you would have had the guts to and own up to your the shit," I said irately.

He interrupted me, "Whoa! What the fuck was my mistake?"

"You slept with my best friend and that doesn't seem like a mistake to you?" I said sarcastically.

"Have you lost your fucking mind!" he yelled like I had never heard him before. "Whom did I sleep with? Your best friend is here with you. Ask her if I ever touched her."

"I am not talking about her. It's about Priyanka," I cried.

"Are you out of your mind, Amy?" he shouted angrily.

"You cannot cover the truth with your loud voice. I saw it with my own eyes. You were in the bed, sleeping with Piu. Both of you were nude and..." my voice choked and I started crying before completing the sentence.

"Waah! Just anything. You dump me and now you're cooking up stories in your defense. You are awesome, Amyra," he said and started clapping sarcastically.

Bam! I slapped Shashank with all energy. "Yeah, I dumped you, Shashank. But you were the reason for it. I did what any dignified girl would have done. Now, be a man. Own up your mistake, so that I may have a little respect for you."

There was pin drop silence for the next few minutes after which I said, "It was a mistake coming here. Let's go Oli."

We got up and started walking towards the door when he shouted from behind, "Ask your friend Priyanka if I ever touched her. If she says so in front of me, I will do anything you ask me."

"We are not on talking terms. But I suppose your best buddy can definitely clarify stuff for me!" I said sarcastically.

"Okay! If you want this, I will call him right now," he said.

"I sure want this. Let's not stretch it anymore," I said rigidly.

He went inside and then came out after a couple of minutes. "He will be here in an hour."

I looked at Oli. She nodded in agreement and I said, "Okay then, we will wait."

24

Extracts from *Love, Loss and Pain*

14 January 2018

9:30 a.m.

I woke and sat up with an awful headache. My ass was completely whacked and every joint in my body seemed wedged. My muscles refused to move as I tried to get off the bed.

"What the fuck! You shouldn't have drank so much, you asshole!" I reprimanded myself for being the pig that I had become last night.

I looked around and realised I was in mom's bedroom.

'How and why on Earth was I in her bedroom?' I tried to think hard, but my memory had turned into a starless new moon night.

Suddenly, the world around me started circling and I became utterly nauseous. I got up from the bed immediately and ran, using all my will power to reach the washroom, but fell face down. My hand hit a couple of cosmetic and other items placed on mom's dressing table that rattled down noisily. My body forsook me miserably and I puked all over the floor.

My arm and shoulder hit the floor hard and I shouted, "Aaah!"

Anurag came running into the room as I tried to get up and slipped on my own expel with a thud. "Damn! Are you okay?" he said and checked on me.

"I don't think so," I replied and puked again.

"Let's get you to the washroom," he said and supported me to reach there.

I cleared my stomach for a couple of more times as he stood, holding my spew-soiled hand. He rubbed my back and said, "I will get some water. Can you stand by yourself?"

"Yeah," I said and went on for some more of it.

I walked out of the washroom, feeling slightly better after the spill. Anurag entered the room, handed me a glass of water and said covering his nose, "Yuck, you stinky fellow! Clean yourself and the room also."

He walked out immediately and I realised that the room needed to be cleaned right then, but I was in no condition. So, I gulped in the water and sauntered wearily to my room.

I went to the washroom, got rid of my grubby clothes and stood under the cold shower. The tiny droplets of wintry water extinguished the intense heat in my body. I left the room slightly rejuvenated and reached the sitting area through the kitchen with a bottle of cold water in my hand.

"Fuck! What the hell is this?" I exclaimed, looking at the dire condition of the sitting room.

The sight amplified the poundings in my head and made me feel dizzy again. Empty disposable glasses and plates with eatables were lying everywhere; the floor was soiled with water and alcohol; rice, pieces of nan, shards of chicken and other foodstuff spread all across the place, including the sofa and the table. There wasn't a place left where I could have sat down comfortably. Anurag managed to find a sweet spot to sit on the sofa as I struggled to find my way to walk through all that mess.

"What the fuck happened here last night, Anu?" I asked.

"No idea, bro," he replied.

"And where are Amy and Priyanka?" I asked, making some place to sit on the other sofa.

"They left earlier—"

"Yeah, they had to get home early," I interrupted him.

"Yess," he hissed as I downed three quarters of the bottle in a go.

I tried to call Amy many times while trying to dig into the incidents of last night with Anu, but her phone was unexpectedly switched off.

"We have work to do, bro!" Anu said.

"I know," I said irritated at the very thought of it.

"Do we have lemon in the kitchen?" I asked him.

"I don't think so. The last one was used by Amyra this morning," he replied.

"Okay," I said and gulped the remaining water in the bottle.

"It's already past ten, bro! We need to clean the whole fucking house, especially aunty's bedroom before she comes back," he said, while getting up and moving towards the kitchen.

"Yes brother!" I agreed while getting my heavy ass off the sofa.

Anurag came back with a broom in his hand and started cleaning the sitting area.

"I will start with mom's bedroom," I said and walked towards the stench-filled battlefield.

We swept and mopped the whole house, disposed all of last night's debris, changed the sofa covers and bed sheets, opened the windows and sprayed air freshener all around to take care of any remnant odour.

It was past noon already, so Anurag went to Anna's, a south Indian restaurant close to my house, to get some idli and vada while I prepared tea for us.

It was then that the two victorious warriors sat down to get some rest, after over an hour of gruelling cleaning session. We enjoyed the tasty breakfast on a shipshape sitting area, admiring our impeccable work.

"Good job!" I said, putting the last crumb of idli in my mouth.

"Thank you," Anu replied sipping his tea.

"I was saying that to myself." I grinned.

"Go, get cleaned! You look like shit," he said, looking at me from the corner of his eyes.

"I look better than you," I replied.

"In your dreams." He laughed.

I smirked and tried calling Amy again. It still said, "The number you are trying to call is switched off."

"Why is her phone switched off?" I said looking towards him.

"How would I know?" He questioned back.

"Yeah," I said while still trying to call her.

"I need to tell you something, bro."

"Yes Anu, I am all ears," I said, while dropping her a text message over WhatsApp.

"It's over!"

"What is over?" His words caught my attention and I turned towards him.

"I mean, you won't be able to reach her."

"Why?" I asked anxiously.

"Coz she dumped you, dammit!" Anurag said heavily.

"Dumped? Why? How? She didn't say anything to me," I said doubtfully.

"I get it. You are trying to mess with me, right?" I giggled and continued, "It is not going to work, bro!"

I tried to call her again and again unsuccessfully.

"You can try as much as you want, Shashank. She is gone," he said rigidly.

He had started getting onto my nerves. "Just shut the fuck up, Anu! This isn't funny anymore."

"I am not kidding. She told me that before she left," he said.

"What did she tell you?" I pulled him by his collar and asked.

"She told me to tell you that it was over between you guys."

"But why?" I got absolutely bewildered and continued, "Everything were beautiful until last night."

"She was just using you for her academics, financials and physical pleasure, I guess. All her classes and internal assessments are over now. She got a lot of expensive gifts from you. Imagine, a lowly middle class girl going around lavish hotels in a fancy car. But now, she doesn't need you anymore, bro. She is all set to go out for her post-graduation. She will find a new prey... or maybe has already found one," he said, trying to hug me.

"You are lying! It just doesn't add up." I got away from him and said restlessly.

I tried calling her again but it still said, "The number you are trying to call is switched off."

"No no! This cannot happen," I said, impatiently while trying to reach Olive and Priyanka. Even, they weren't responding to my calls.

"What the fuck is happening!" I dropped in text after text into their WhatsApp accounts.

They seemed to have blocked me because I was unable to see any of their DPs or status.

"What did she tell you, bro?" I had tears dripping down my eyes by then.

"I told you buddy, she cleverly manipulated you. And now that she doesn't need you anymore, she was not ready to carry on this relationship anymore," he said.

"It cannot be so, Anu. Not again," I said and started crying bitterly.

"I gave the best to her. She cannot do this to me. There is a mistake, some misunderstanding. I have to clear it out. I need to talk to her," I said and continued, "I will go to her house and sort it out with her. I will apologise for any mistake that I might have committed. We just need to talk, and it will be good," I said.

Anurag tried to stop me, but I didn't give a shit to what he said and left immediately.

It took me much longer due to high traffic congestion before I reached her house and knocked the door a few times, with no response. Doubts started creeping into my mind, turning me restless and I started banging the door, "Amy! Open up the door!"

Finally, the door opened after a few minutes. It was her mom.

"Hello ma'am. Is Amy home?" I asked politely.

"No, she isn't," she replied coldly and closed the door.

I knew she was home and started banging the door again.

She opened once again and asked angrily, "What's your problem? What do you want?"

"I need to talk to Amy, just once. Please!" I pleaded.

"Don't you understand she isn't home! Go away and don't disturb," she said and shut the door on my face.

I started banging the door again and shouted, "I know she is inside. Please open up, ma'am, please."

She opened the door and gave me a tight slap, "Why are you bothering us? I told you she isn't home. Even if she was, there was no way she would talk to you Shashank."

I was flabbergasted to hear my name from her. She knew me, which meant that she also knew about us.

"I just want to know why she wouldn't talk to me. I love her. I need to talk to her, even if for a minute. Please ma'am. I beg of you. Please," I said with folded hands.

"Don't you understand the meaning of NO. Just get the hell out or I will call the police," she said harshly.

People started gathering around the gate and a couple of boys came near the door and asked, "What happened aunty? Is this person bothering you?"

I was infuriated at their interference and said, "It's our matter and I would suggest that you stay out of it."

"This person has been troubling Amyra since a long time and now he has followed her here. I was just telling him that we will call the police if he doesn't stop stalking her," her mom said rigidly.

A number of boys came by then and one of them said, "There is no need to call the police, aunty. We will take care of him."

They surrounded me. Two of them caught me from behind and dragged me out of the house's premises as I continued pleading, "I just want to talk to her once, ma'am, please."

Her mom had already closed the door and eight guys stood in front of me.

"It's no more your matter, bro!" One of them said and they started advancing.

"There's no need for any of this," I said, while trying to retract.

One of the big guys, who seemed like the leader, tried to attack me and I defended myself, reflexively punching him hard.

He fell down, grinding his teeth in pain while others pounced on me instantly and I fell down on the pitch road. They stomped my body, my legs and my hands continuously from all sides as I cried in pain. I tried to defend myself for some time, but my body gave up soon. Things had become cold and dark for me by then. I did not feel pain anymore.

The leader had recovered by then and he told them to hold me up for him. Bam! He punched me hard and I groaned out loud in pain. I fell down as they left me.

"Pick him up again!" I heard an indistinct voice and felt some of them picking me up again. Bam! It was a right hook punch on my face and I fell face down immediately. Everything turned hazy. All I could get was the taste and smell of my blood in my mouth and nose.

The faint words of some heavenly soul echoed in my ears, "Go away! Are you going to kill him?"

After that, they left me lying on the road. A blurred image of a grey-haired old man appeared in front of my eyes. He asked, "Can you get up?"

"I think so!" I tried to get up with his help. Every part of my body stung me hard. I spit out blood from my mouth. I had had a big cut somewhere in my tongue or cheek. My nose bled unceasingly.

The good samaritan helped me sit beside the road and asked, "Is there something I can do for you?"

"I am good, sir. Thank you very much!" I said and got up after a few minutes.

One of the guys came back from somewhere as I limped towards my car and threatened, "We are going to kill you next time."

I did not have the energy to retaliate and got into the car and drove towards my house weeping bitterly. However, the pain in my body was infinitesimal as compared to that in my heart.

At around 3:00 p.m., when I got back home, Anurag asked the moment he saw me. "What the fuck happened, man?"

"Nothing!" I said trying to hide my pain.

"You have been pounded heavily," he said.

"Yeah, kind of!" I said as he supported me to reach the living room.

"I am gonna kill that bitch," he shouted.

"It wasn't her fault. I don't think she even knows about it," I tried to defend her.

"Whatever man. How many?" he asked.

"I am not sure, may be eight," I said while sitting down on the sofa.

"Let's get to the hospital before mom sees you like this," he said.

"Okay," I said coughing.

"You should register an FIR." He was infuriated.

"Against whom? Amy, the girl I love? Not happening, dude," I said trying to gulp in my pain.

"Yes, and I think I should have told you in the morning," he said.

His words turned my head towards him in a jerk, "There is something else?"

"She tried to hit on me," he said looking straight into my eyes..

"Does it really mean that she—?" I asked nervously.

"Yes!" he interrupted me.

"So, did you guys..?" I was already in tears.

"No buddy, I would never betray you." He hugged me, but my world had already turned upside down and I started bewailing furiously. Things had taken an unbelievable turn in my life. He tried to console me, but I was beyond that.

That was the last thing I had expected of her. I tried to get in touch with her for the next few months in all the ways possible, but failed massively. She blocked me from everywhere and did not respond to my mails. She left the town and went away to an unknown place. I did not know what to think or what to do; but I was sure of two things – she had dumped me in the worst possible way and my life would never be the same again.

My eyes gawked at the wilderness of dreams,
Your voices filled my head; absolute obscurity.
"Our togetherness shall last up to this day,"
The reverie of church bell, folks, was smashed to smithereens.
My heart twinged, the destiny of my true love; murky?
Akin to mirage, you drifted away, I wailed in agony,
I jigged; clenched you with arrant thew,
Vibe of free fall embraced, gravity preeminent,
Wind smacked my body, eyes faced opacity.
The journey charmed, no trepidation besieged as I cascaded.
A congenial cloud of love engulfed; absolute obscurity.

The End

25

The Treacherous Witness

2 January 2019

11:30 a.m.

The uncomfortable silence was broken by the doorbell that echoed through the house.

Shashank got up to get the door saying, "He is here." We could hear them talk indistinctly as he opened the door.

"What's the emergency?" he asked completely unaware of our presence.

"This!" Shashank said and pointed towards us as they reached near the sitting area.

"Hi Anurag!" I said, waving my hand. He froze at our sight and his eyes turned visibly bland.

"Hi Amyra!" he replied in a shaky voice after a minute.

Anurag's reaction on seeing us confused me a little. The look on Shashank's face seemed perplexing too. "I expected a better reaction than this!" I said with a taunt.

"Oh, sorry! Just didn't expect to see you guys," he said trying to get back his composure.

"Whatever!" I said uncaringly.

"How are you?" he asked.

"I am good and will be much better after you answer my question in front of Shashank," I replied looking sternly towards Shashank.

"What question?" he asked nervously.

"Your best friend has written a book. I suppose you are well aware of it. He claims it to be a true story. So I would like to ask you a few things."

"Okay!" he answered nervously.

"Did I ever proclaim, or give you all an impression that I was exploiting Shashank for academic benefits?" I asked him.

"No," he answered.

"Did you ever feel, or any of my friends told you that I needed him for financial gains or physical pleasure?"

"No."

"Finally, did I try to hit on you?" I shot him with my final question.

"No," he denied, reaching the peak of his nervousness and wiping beads of sweat on his forehead that had sprung up inadvertently on a cold winter day.

I looked at Shashank who had already turned pale and jittery by then. "Fuck man, you lied to me!" He held Anurag's collar and started crying fervently.

"How could you do this to me," his voice choked completely.

"I am sorry, brother," he replied with tears in his eyes.

"Don't call me brother!" Shashank shouted looking at him and came near me.

"I am really very sorry. Please forgive me." He fell down on his knees with folded hands and cried.

"It's okay," I said with tears in my eyes.

"Sorry, sorry..." he continued pleading.

"It's okay, Shashank. Please stop it!" I had started crying vehemently by then too.

"Don't cry, Amy..." He wiped the tears from my face and continued, "Everything is my fault. Maybe, I slept with Priyanka..."

"Yes, you did, Shashank!"

"I am sorry. Maybe, my friend told me lies about you to prevent me dying of guilt." Shashank was inconsolable.

"Yeah, maybe." I didn't know what else to say.

"I am sorry. I wish you all the very best for everything. Bye, Amyra," he said and turned away from me.

"It's okay, Shashank. Thank you. I wish you the same. Bye," I said and started walking towards the door with a heavy heart and teary eyes.

I had never thought that walking away from him would be that difficult. I had to push myself hard for each step ahead.

"It wasn't even Shashank's fault, Amyra," Anurag said loudly.

I turned around reflexively at his words and exclaimed, "What!"

He turned his gaze away as I looked into his eyes.

I walked up to him and asked, "What do you mean, Anurag?"

"I mean, he is innocent," Anurag said and burst into tears.

I was completely flummoxed, not knowing what to think or believe.

"But you saw it with your own eyes. He is just trying to defend his friend. Let's go, Amy!" Oli said, looking into my eyes. She had a valid point, but my heart was not ready to leave.

"Tell me what happened that night, Anurag," I said looking into his eyes.

Shashank stood right there, staring at him blankly.

"And I need to know only the truth," I said.

Anurag started speaking.

13 January 2018

We went for a drive towards the highway after dropping Olive home on Priyanka's suggestion with the idea to give you guys some more private time. Approximately ten kilometres outside the city, she said, "Anurag, can you pull over?"

"Here?" I asked surprised.

"Yes, I need to step out and get some fresh air," she replied.

"I can switch off the AC and lower the windows, if you want," I said, while turning down the volume of music..

"My feet seem numb. I need to move around a bit, if it's not too much trouble for you," she requested.

"That's not a problem. It's just that the area is deserted at this time," I said.

"Okay!" she said dolefully.

Puppy eyes! I looked at them and became the victim of her emotional manipulation. "It's okay, I am good," she said as I pulled over at a safe spot, away from the speeding vehicles.

I turned off the ignition and said, "Let's go!"

"Are you sure it's okay for you?" she asked.

"Oh yes, now please, can we move out?" I replied with folded hands.

"Okay!" She chirped and hopped down immediately.

Cold wind made me shiver instantaneously and I rubbed my hands to generate some heat. "Why the fuck did she have to get out of the car at this time?" I looked around and said to myself, feeling irritated.

The place was dimly illuminated by the half-moon and the accompanying stars. Occasional breezes made the trees and bushes on the sides of the road rustle softly. I looked at Priyanka, who strolled uncaringly. She seemed completely unfettered by the cold weather.

Something happened at that moment and my eyes got fixed on her smooth legs drenched by the soft beams of the moon. She put the tresses that came to her eyes behind the ears as the wind blew.

"What?" she asked me.

"Nothing," I said embarrassed, because she had caught me staring at her.

"I know what you were up to, Anurag," she said walking closer to me.

"It's nothing Priyanka," I said stepping back away from her.

"All men are the same," she said.

"Sorry! But you are getting me all wrong," I said apologetically.

"Am I really getting you wrong Anurag?" she said while still coming closer to me.

"Yes," I replied and realised that my lower back was against the hood of my car.

She was uncomfortably close to me by then. I could feel her warm breath and said, "Priyanka—"

Her lips scraped against mine before I could complete my sentence and she put her finger on my lips whispering, "Shhhh."

I was shocked and said, "Are—"

"Shut the fuck up!" She interrupted me seductively and our lips mashed each other's within moments. We worked our mouth as our tongues battled furiously for minutes.

"Fuck me!" she said.

I was shaken from head to toe and stared at her blankly as the words ricocheted in my ears.

"You heard me right. I want you to fuck me," she said alluringly.

"But..." Her cold hands found their way inside my clothes before I could say anything further. Her actions were irresistibly sensual and I gave in immediately. I crushed Payal's trust mercilessly inside the car that evening to satisfy my lust without an iota of guilt in my heart.

We clicked a lot of pics that evening, especially during and after the act.

"I hope you had a good time, Anurag," she said as we drove back.

"Yesss…" I hissed and continued. "You were amazing. I hope you were not disappointed by me!"

"C'mon! Didn't my moans and groans convey enough?" She grinned and blushed.

"You would have been louder if the car was bigger!" I said proudly.

"Don't worry, Anurag! You are going to give me a hell lot of pleasure," she said.

She was turning me on again.

"Is this gonna continue?" I asked excitedly.

"I will do anything you want, if you give me what I need." She winked at me wickedly.

"So what does Priyanka need? Multiple orgasms?" I said impishly.

"I have some other G-spots and want you to fiddle with them." Her voice turned inexplicably smoky.

She had turned me on again and I wanted to jump in between her legs immediately. I slowed down and said, "God, you are so irresistible. Should we go for another round?"

She smiled and said, "You want me to reach cloud nine?"

"Oh yes!" I said and pulled over.

"Send our pics to your girlfriend right now!" she said.

I was taken aback by her words but I said, "You are kidding, right?"

"Do I sound like that?" she said with a shock.

"If this is a joke, I want you to stop it right now."

"I am in no mood for a joke, but definitely wanna fuck you!" she said touching herself.

I watched her clueless as she continued, "I gave *you* what *you* wanted, Anurag," she said. "And now you are going to give me what *I* want."

"What do you want?" She was testing my patience.

"I already told you. Send our pics," she reiterated.

"What the fuck!" I had started to lose my cool by then.

"Shhh. Keep your voice low!" She put finger on my lips and said sarcastically, "You gave me one heck of a fuck and promised me more pleasure, so give it to me now."

She started radiating intense negative vibes. I was exasperated and tried to snatch the phone from her.

"Hey stop, don't act like an uneducated brat," she said and handed over the phone to me saying. "Take it, and break it into pieces! The pics are already saved on the cloud."

She really was on to something evil and I knew that I was completely fucked up and asked, "What do you want?"

"Now we are talking," she said with an atrocious smile.

"Just say it!" I yelled.

"Don't get overexcited. All I need is your help to separate the the two love birds."

"What do you mean?" I asked nervously.

"Don't act like you don't understand," she said with an annoying smile.

"I really don't understand what you are trying to say," I clarified.

"Okay! If that's how you want to play, I will simplify it for you. You will help me split Shashank and Amyra."

"What!" I yelled in horror.

"Yes," she replied.

My hands and legs turned ice cold as I said, "Why? She is your best friend."

"Best friend, my foot!" she shouted furiously. "She is nothing but a stinking asshole!"

"Maybe she isn't your friend, but Shashank is my buddy, and I can't do that to him!" I spoke out loud.

"Oh really! Are you ready to serve jail term just for your friendship?" she said like a classic vamp.

"Wh.... What?" I gulped in some air through the extremely parched throat.

"You know, your semen in still in here," she said pointing downwards. "A perfect proof for the rape charges."

"Bitch!" I said and slapped her and realised my mistake immediately.

"Ouch!" She shouted. "Unlock the fucking door, Anurag." She could have opened the door herself, but she did not. However, I was unable to understand that then. "The highway patrol party is right here. Now, I will put rape and battery charges on you. And you are going to lose everything, you fucker!"

I saw a vehicle of the cops nearing us right away and was shaken to the soul. I started pleading with folded hands, "I am really sorry."

"Bam, bam, bam, bam!" She slapped me four times, but I was relieved that the cops passed us. The fear made those slaps feel like a soft feathery touch and I continued apologising.

"It's okay. I think we are done with all of this drama," she said.

"Sorry! But, how can I do this to my best friend?" I cried.

"Okay, so you want to stretch it? Then, let's see what Payal has to say about these," she said while waving the mobile in her hand, showcasing the pics.

"Here, I found her!" She said waving her mobile that had Payal's Facebook page.

"No, stop!" I cried loudly.

"So, are you going to help me?" she asked.

"Do I have a choice?" I said dejectedly.

"Of course, yes!" She laughed wickedly and continued, "You have two choices – you can be faithful to your friend and lose everything; your love, respect, business and serve jail. Or you can help me and keep all of the above. The choice is yours."

I stayed mum for a few minutes.

"We don't have the whole night, Mr Anurag Singh. Do you need some motivation?" she said looking at the phone.

"Okay, I will do it!" I said helplessly.

"Bravo! You have made the right decision and won a chance to get kissed by me again," she said and stooped over.

I stopped her and said, "Stay away, you bitch!"

"That's rude," she said and retracted.

"What do you want me to do now?" I asked sternly.

"I want you to ensure putting this in the drinks of our lovers and make them fully drunk tonight," she said and showed me a silver-coloured blister packed medicine.

The label said, "Alprazolam 10."

"What is this?" I asked.

"Just a simple sleeping pill," she said plainly.

"But why?"

"Coz I want to get Shashank drunk and fuck him," she said and smiled maliciously.

I was appalled at her evil intentions and said, "But why do you want to do this?"

"That's none of your business. Just do what you are asked to, and a big reward awaits!" she said and kissed my ear.

"Please don't make me do this!" I pleaded.

"Oh! You are such a baby." She combed her finger through my hair and said ostentatiously, "Let's get going. I cannot wait for my next orgasm."

26

Anurag's story: Who needs foes?

14 January 2018

2:30 a.m.

Shashank was on his ninth peg, whereas Amyra was on her sixth. Priyanka and I were on a much lower side at a mere second. I had ensured getting you people drunk, as I kept pouring water in our drinks.

Priyanka put one of the pills in Shashank's drink when the two of you went to the washroom together and I had to watch Shashank gulp in the last peg helplessly. The two of you lay motionless on the sofa right in front of our eyes within minutes.

"C'mon, honey! It's time for some quick action," Priyanka said after seeing your condition.

"What do you want me to do?" I asked angrily.

"Fuck me!" she stepped near and kissed my lips.

I grabbed her hair and said, "Do you want my help or not?"

"Ouch! I am not BDSM type!" she said.

I looked at her hatefully as she directed, "Dump your ex-bhabhi into Shashank's bedroom."

"And?" I asked.

"You will know everything with time babe!" she said.

"I am not your babe." I yelled.

"Okay honey. Get going! We have more work to do," she spoke with a simper.

I did what she asked me to.

"And now, we need to get Shashank to the other room," she said when I got back.

"Which room?" I asked.

"Any other room. I think his mother's bedroom will be good," she said after thinking for a few seconds.

"I cannot carry him alone," I expressed my inability.

"Don't worry, I am here," she chirped gleefully.

We then carried Shashank to his mother's room and put him on the bed.

"This morning shall be a turning point in everyone's life here," Priyanka said proudly.

"So, we are done here?" I said.

"Not even close, honey. You have a major role to play. Things have just started." Her voice was filled with hatred.

"What's more?" I asked nervously.

"So this is what's gonna happen in the morning. When your sweet bhabhi gets up, she will find me sleeping with your best friend."

"Please don't do this!" I cried.

"Calm down. You have no part to play in that. I trust my best friend to find it all by herself and leave your friend immediately." She continued after a brief pause, "Well, before she leaves, she will leave you a message for Shashank."

"So you want me to be the messenger now?" I said.

"Exactly! Except that the message shall be mine," she said with that sordid grin on her face.

"And what shall that be?" I asked.

"You will tell Shashank that Amyra had used him only for her academic, financial and physical needs. Now that her graduation and assessments neared completion and she planned to go out for further studies, he was becoming a useless burden," she said plainly.

"Don't you think the reason is far less convincing, owing to the depth of their relationship?" I asked in doubt.

"Yes, you are absolutely right. But, you are forgetting the fact that Shashank has been dumped in a similar manner before, so it won't be too difficult for him to accept it as a recurring pattern in his life. Amy told me about it long back and I knew it would be a perfect weapon for me. However, in order to ensure things go our way, your role becomes very crucial. You will have to convince him somehow, or else you know the consequences," she said.

I stared at her quizzically as she continued, "You will also tell him that Amyra tried to hit on you. In fact, it would be more fun if you tell him that you fucked her."

"I can't do that. He is my only friend," I said with folded hands.

"I would now suggest you get some rest. You need to get up before your bhabhi."

"You disgust me Priyanka," I said and turned around.

"Don't lock the room. I want Amy to enter easily." She ignored my words and shouted as I left the room.

And, the next morning, things fell into place exactly as she had planned and all of you now know the rest.

2 January 2019 / Present Day

12:30 p.m.

There was pin drop silence in the house. All of us were in a state of shock. "I know my actions don't deserve forgiveness," Anurag broke the silence.

I took a step towards him and the room echoed with a tight slap.

"I am sorry. I was scared." He folded his hands and started crying vehemently.

"Your actions turned our lives into living hell. Do you have any idea what I have been through in the last one year?" I yelled at the top of my voice and continued slapping him.

"I know. I am so sorry, Amyra." He went down on his knees.

"You're sorry? Can you bring back the lost time? Erase the pain that I went through?" I was still shouting. "You were the one who betrayed your girlfriend and made us pay for it. How is it fair, Anurag?" I wanted to kick him, but Shashank held me back.

"How could he do that to us, Shashank?" I said, still trying to reach Anurag.

"It's okay," Shashank said.

"No!" I shouted.

"Just look at me," Shashank said and turned me towards himself.

I stood still, looking into his love-filled eyes as he continued, "It's okay baby."

I couldn't resist any further and hugged him tight. The two of us started crying fervently.

"I am sorry!" Shashank managed to find a way through his choked throat after a few minutes.

"It wasn't your fault," I replied amidst sobs.

"I love you, Amy."

There was no way I could have held back. "I love you too Shashank!"

"I missed you a lot," he said and burst into tears again.

"Me too," I replied while trying to get over my whimper.

Shashank then turned towards Anurag and picked him up by his shoulder.

"I am sorry, Shashank. I don't deserve your friendship," he said wiping his face.

"Yes, you are right. You don't deserve me, but you are my only friend in this world, and I don't have a fucking choice," Shashank said and hugged him.

"Why did she do it?" Oli shot a mind-boggling question towards Anurag.

"I don't know," he answered blankly.

"Okay then, I suppose only one person has the answers to our questions. Let's pay a grand visit to the master planner!" I said sarcastically.

"Is it even necessary? We are good. Isn't it?" Shashank asked.

"No Shashank. I considered that bitch as my best friend and she backstabbed me ruthlessly. I want to know why," I said indignantly.

"Me too!" Oli seconded me.

"Okay," Shashank said.

"Can you give me five minutes?" Anurag said heavily. All our eyes turned towards him as he continued, "I need to plead myself guilty to Payal."

"Are you sure buddy?" Shashank asked.

"Yes, I need to come clean. I cannot live with this shit anymore," he said.

"You are right. It's better she gets to know it from you rather than someone else," I said.

"I am so scared!" His voice choked, overwhelmed by negative apprehensions as he walked towards the door to make his life-altering call.

A single thought echoed in my mind, "With friends like them, who needs foes!"

2:00 p.m.

Priyanka's voice hit our ears after thirty long seconds of knocking. "Who's there?"

"It's me!" Oli replied.

She opened the door after a brief pause and said with a smile, "Hi, old gang!"

There was not a fleck of guilt or grief on her radiant face. She was in her regular pink t-shirt and printed pyjamas.

"I see everyone's here!" She chuckled.

I slapped her and said, "You can smile now, bitch."

"That's so sweet of you, Amy!" she said with an atrocious smile.

She looked at Anurag and said, "Your game is over."

"I already told her everything, you slut," he said gravely.

"Aww! So sad! I am so sorry that she left you, honey," she said, showing fake consolation.

"You know what, I may be suffering a lot because of my breakup, but I am relieved to get rid of the guilt that had been killing me every day. And, I am glad to be with my true friend who I betrayed because of you."

Shashank took a step and stood by his side while I asked Priyanka, "Why?"

"I feel so sorry for you, Anu baby," she said ignoring my question.

I went closer to her and said, "I need an answer, Piu. Why did you do this to me? We were best friends."

"Friends!" she said and started laughing furiously.

"What's so funny?" Oli asked.

"Friends are supposed to support one another in dark times. Friends are supposed to trust one another. Friends are supposed to love one another. And, friends don't backbite. Isn't it, Amy?" she said looking at me.

"Right, and these things sound absurd coming from you," I replied.

"Just quit beating around the bush and come to the point," Oli seemed to be losing her patience.

"You guys remember Mayank?" she asked looking at the two of us.

The name shrouded me with a blanket of nostalgia. I drifted back to our school days when life used to be carefree. There wouldn't be a soul in this world who will not be willing to trade all his belongings to live those days recurrently.

We studied in ninth standard when this person came into our lives, specifically Piu's life. It would not be an exaggeration to say that he was her greatest stalker ever!

27

Her Tireless Stalker

5 June 2012

5:30 p.m.

The three of us were out for a leisurely walk in a small local garden that had nothing, but a few wild bushes, when a familiar voice echoed from behind, "Hi Priyanka!"

We turned around to find Mayank, the person who had been following Piu for the last seven months. He was a dark slender boy with curly hair and black eyes, dressed in a multi-coloured t-shirt and grey jeans. He was a student of Seth Sitaram College, probably in the first year.

"Hey, it's you again!" Piu replied in an 'I don't give a fuck' tone.

"Yes," he answered with a innocent smile.

"Why do you keep following me? I don't like it," she interrupted rudely.

"I just need your answer," he said.

"I already told you a hundred times. It's a big NO."

"But why? Am I not worthy of your love?" His voice was dejected, yet confident.

"It is not that, Mayank. I just don't feel anything for you. We can be friends, as I have told you a million times, but—"

"Friendship, my ass! I love you and I need you to love me back at any cost," he yelled, drawing a lot of attention towards us.

"Have you completely lost your mind?" I jumped into Piu's defence immediately.

"Yes," he continued shouting.

"Don't create a scene over here Mayank!" Piu said angrily, looking around from the corners of her eyes.

"Please accept my love. Be mine," he started pleading on his knees.

"Just stop it!" Piu yelled.

"Is there any problem, girls?" One of the men walked up to us and asked.

"No uncle, we are fine," Oli replied.

"It seems he is bothering you," he said, staring sternly into Mayank's eyes.

He panicked and ran away immediately.

"Thank you, uncle!" Piu said.

"You are welcome. We are right here if he comes back," he said pointing towards his group standing at a distance.

"Let's get out of here, Piu!" I said.

"Yes," she answered and we started walking hastily.

"Give me the final answer, Priyanka." We were startled to hear it again, the moment we stepped out of the garden.

"Don't you fucking understand? It was, it is and it will always be a big no!" Piu shouted back.

The three of us rushed back home as he continued to shout from behind, "My life is meaningless and I prefer to end it without you Priyanka. I love you!"

We ignored his words. However, what followed next morning was an unexpected madness.

6 June 2012

7:00 a.m.

My eyes opened to an unusual commotion early in the morning. I was still figuring out what the matter was, when mom entered the room and said hurriedly, "Amy get up! Olive is here."

"What happened, ma?"

Oli entered the room before I could have finished my sentence. "Mayank killed himself last night," she said anxiously.

"What?" I shouted in disbelief and all the lethargy left me instantly.

Oli continued, "He mentioned Piu's name in his suicide note."

"What?" It was mom's turn to react now.

I did not know what to say.

"Police is interrogating Piu and her mom," Oli said.

"Who was Mayank and what did Piu have to do with him?" Mom asked.

"I will tell you later, mom. Let's go to Piu's house now!" I jumped out of the bed immediately and left.

A bunch of cops were leaving the house when we reached. We could hear people moving around and murmuring a lot of stuff outside her house. They had found an excellent topic for spicy gossip for days to come. We got inside to find her covered in tears and sitting on a chair with her mom beside her in the first room.

We went closer to her and I said, "Hey Piu!"

She jumped up, hugged the two of us tight and started wailing inconsolably, the moment my voice hit her ears.

"Everything's going to be okay," Oli said, patting her back.

"He died. He killed himself. And everybody thinks I am the one responsible." She cried consistently.

"Don't cry Piu," I said, wiping her tears.

"He slashed his veins... and inked the note in his blood!" Her voice choked as she struggled through every word amongst the hiccups. Images of him speaking to Piu floated around my head and turned me empathetic. Tears started rolling out of my eyes.

She continued after a brief pause, "I saw the letter... and puked."

"Shit!" I felt dizzy, just listening to that shit.

My mom brought her a glass of water while aunty showed us the pic of the blood-soiled suicide note in her mobile. It seemed like a page from one of his single-lined college notebooks. It had impressions of his thumb and other fingers in the form of blood stains all over.

The page was filled from top to bottom by a note written perceptively from a shivering finger that said, "PRIYANKA, I LUV U. I CAN'T LIVE WITHOUT U. GUD BYE"

Goosebumps erupted across my body.

28

She turned the tables?

2 January 2019, Present Day

2:15 p.m.

"Did you guys really forget him?" Piu's question brought me back to the present.

"No, I remember him well. But what does that have to do with this?" I questioned her back.

"Well! You know everybody blamed me for his death?"

"Yes! But what are you trying to say?" I asked in an irritated voice.

"Everyone, *including you guys*," she said, stressing the last three words.

"Are you out of your mind?" I shouted.

"We stood by you all the time, Piu. I think your memory is failing you," Oli said.

"Quit doing the things you are unqualified for!" Piu said eyeballing, Oli sarcastically.

"You are making no sense!" I said.

"It will make sense in a minute," she said.

"I am all ears!"

Piu started narrating

A week after that incident, I went to Oli's house to find the two of you sitting in the veranda. Your backs were turned towards me, so I tiptoed slowly behind the bush to startle you guys. However, I held myself back naively, and thankfully so, the moment Amy spelled out my name.

A drop of tear rolled down my left eye as Amy said, "I feel it was definitely Piu's fault. She enjoyed every bit of his attention and when Mayank sought commitment, she repudiated him in the most discourteous manner."

Oli supported you, "I think you are right!"

Amy said, "I don't know if you realised, but there has been a radical change in her dressing style and the amount of makeup that she has started wearing in the last few months. She probably did all of it for him."

Oli answered, "I am able to connect the dots."

Amy continued, "I feel bad for Mayank and his parents. She did not deserve his love. Now, she moves around telling everybody it wasn't her fault."

I did not have the guts to hear anything else and walked away in tears, without giving you guys a hint of my presence.

You people were supposed to be my world; the only ones I loved and trusted with all my heart and you smashed it to smithereens.

I considered you my best friends. I was so wrong. You were not even my friends. You turned out to be worse than everyone else around me. You stabbed me in the back ruthlessly and killed our friendship that day.

Do you guys have any idea how it felt to visit police stations every now and then, just to give the same answer again and again? Why did I dump him? Why did I egg him to commit suicide? What was the depth of our relationship? What exactly happened that forced him to take such a step? Did we have a fight over something? If yes, when did the fight happen? Were we physical? If yes, up to what extent? Did I ever hang out with him? How many guys had I been with till then? How many guys I had fucked? Why should they not put a murder charge on me.... and the questions continued in front of my mom. You don't have any fucking idea how tortured my mom and I were. Moreover, the way that cop touched me still gives me goose bumps. I literally trembled and ended up shitting in my pant out of fear in the police station; adding to my embarrassment. I started feeling, that everyone else was right. Maybe, I was wrong.

People stared at me with those fucking judgmental eyes, no matter where I went. I was a murderer for everyone. They fired unreasonable allegations that suffocated me inside out.

I was shattered and spent nights crying and staring the walls blankly. The guilt of his death coupled with your betrayal became too much for me to handle.

I used to see Mayank calling me in my dreams. His face and that bloody letter flashed in front of my eyes all the time. I started sharing mom's bed because I could hear him whisper things into my ears at night. It scared me to death.

So, one fine morning, I decided to bring an end to everything, just, like him. I picked up a knife from the kitchen and chafed the sparkling metal lightly on my wrist.

A plethora of thoughts hit me from every dimension, pushing me to the brink when suddenly, mom's voice echoed in my head, "I love you darling! You are the only reason of my existence after your father."

'What the fuck are you doing Piu!' Wisdom dawned on me and I threw the gizmo far away. I jumped into the bed as the knife clamoured on the floor, pressed my face against the pillow and started howling. The cotton faithfully absorbed the noise and my blabbers while getting completely dowsed by my tears. It had been the most loyal friend to me in the darkest of times.

Suddenly, I yelled at myself, "Enough! No more of it!"

I jumped out of the bed resolutely, wiped my tears, stood in front of mirror and spoke to myself looking at it, "It wasn't your fault, Priyanka. Get it etched into your brain. Mayank couldn't handle your rejection and acted cowardly; that's not something you should blame yourself for."

And then, the anger took over. "As for Amyra; I will prepare a poison more formidable than the one that housed in her head. I will make her guzzle it, by hook or by crook. It would be fun to see her cry in agony as the venom tears her apart."

I desperately waited and the harvest of your karma ripened after six long years, giving me a full-fledged opening. There was not a chance that I could have let go of it on that blessed day.

A dark silence engulfed the room as we tried to absorb Priyanka's every spoken word. The thought of her domesticating a grudge and faking friendship for so many years was unbelievable.

She said after a brief pause, "Assuming your 'friend' Anurag has already shared the details, it would not be an exaggeration to say that the whole setup favoured me that evening. Things aligned itself perfectly as per plan with a miniscule effort and I enjoyed every bit of it."

She then turned towards Anurag and said, "Thanks a lot for your help, Anurag. And, you don't need to worry about the pics anymore."

He was fuming. "Shut up!"

"I feel sorry for you now, Anurag. But, I am available," she continued with a smile and shifted her attention towards Shashank. "I am sorry, Shashank sir. Nothing personal. You had to suffer for something you had nothing to do with."

"It was all personal, Piu!" He ground his teeth and replied with fire in his eyes. "You think what they did in your childhood days justifies what you did to her and every one of us now?"

"I don't need to justify anything, Shashank sir," she said sarcastically.

"You are wrong, Priyanka. No matter what you say, you know in your heart that you were wrong. I can see it in your eyes. And if it was inner peace that you were looking for after doing all of this, I wish you find that and you move on," Shashank said and walked out with Anurag.

It was just the three of us now and the only words that set out of my lips were, "I am really sorry, Piu. But we were just kids then. Do you—?"

"Don't, Amy!" Oli interrupted. "You don't owe her an apology. She took her revenge and looks in a great shape. There's nothing left here. Let's just go!"

Piu did not utter a word and pointed us to the door of her house with seemingly no regret on her face.

'How vulnerable is the bond of our love?' I thought to myself as I stepped out of her house 'Subtle and sensitive individuals like us can be agonised even by the smallest grain of suspicion. It should be protected diligently by layers of unbreakable trust and faith to keep it immune from evil-eyed onlookers at all times. But I was stupid enough to allow it to get jolted by a bystander.'

A word to clear the air, just what Shashank was looking for in all these months. It would have purged all evil plots right there. He did not admit, but somewhere I feel that he wrote an entire book so that his words reached me. And then what happened? The book got published!

What more? I read it.

Then? We communicated.

And? Things got sorted.

It may sound unbelievable, but it happened. You know why? Because god favours us, and this imperfect love story is meant to last forever.